"Rainbows are a plus," Mike whispered.

She held the crystal toward the sun. "They make rainbows on the floor every afternoon. But this one's . . . *inside* the quartz," she said dreamily, adding, "You love the crystals, don't you? Just like Granddad does."

A strange look crossed his face. "They get in your blood, Kristy. Like gold. And you keep looking for the perfect one, which you never find."

Her breathing felt ragged. "That's what I felt at the mine. I could have stayed all day—all week. . . ."

His finger traced along the sensitive skin beneath her jaw. "But could you stay for years, Kristy? Does the crystal fire burn that brightly in your blood?"

Her skin felt hot where he touched her. But it wasn't crystal fire that burned in her blood right now. . . .

Marcella Thompson had lived in various parts of the United States but always came back to what she calls her mountains in Arkansas. Finally, she decided to stay. She and her husband, Glenn, raise blueberries, and Marcella works the blueberries during the summer and writes in the winter. They live on a lovely piece of land near Fayetteville with a collection of dogs and cats, all of which she says are "strange and special in their own way."

Books by Marcella Thompson

HARLEQUIN ROMANCE
2802—BREAKING FREE
2975—BED, BREAKFAST & BEDLAM

Don't miss any of our special offers. Write to us at the following address for information on our newest releases.

Harlequin Reader Service
P.O. Box 1397, Buffalo, NY 14240
Canadian address: P.O. Box 603,
Fort Erie, Ont. L2A 5X3

OF RASCALS
AND RAINBOWS

Marcella Thompson

Harlequin Books

TORONTO • NEW YORK • LONDON
AMSTERDAM • PARIS • SYDNEY • HAMBURG
STOCKHOLM • ATHENS • TOKYO • MILAN

ISBN 0-373-03106-8

Harlequin Romance first edition February 1991

For all the crystal diggers,
Then and Now
With special thanks to
The Coleman Quartz Company & Myrna
and to Paula and Penny

OF RASCALS AND RAINBOWS

CHAPTER ONE

KRISTY CUNNINGHAM sat on the terrace, twisting the end of her pigtail around one finger while she contemplated her horoscope in the morning paper. As uninteresting as her horoscope was for that particular day, it was still more interesting than the obscure painters and paintings in the thick art history book that lay unopened in her lap. And it was only the second week of classes. Her roommate, Penny, lay on the chaise in a string bikini, swimming in some oil concoction of her own making.

Kristy tucked an errant strand of thick black hair behind her ear. "Penny?"

"Um?"

"Even my horoscopes have given up on me. Not a glimmer of 'you will find a new enterprise,' or 'challenges lie ahead' for days. Not even a 'dark, mysterious stranger' on the horizon."

She sighed and moved her chair out of the direct sun. Penny turned a lovely golden brown in the hot Texas sun, Kristy turned lobster red and peeled. She took after her mother's side of the family—black hair, blue eyes, fair skin—all of which other people found stunning, but which she found tiresome, given the quality and quantity of the Texas sun. She smeared sunscreen on her nose. "I'm never going to get through this stupid course. I'll be in school until I'm old and gray."

"I told you art history was a bad idea. You don't have the temperament." Penny was in her last year of banking and finance and planned to be a millionaire by age thirty. "And if you read the financial page instead of the horoscopes, you'd be better off."

After five years at the University of Texas in Austin, Kristy was still searching for something to major in. Oh, how she envied Penny and her single-minded devotion to the world of finance. "Well, I don't think it's fair. It's not like I don't have enough hours." She supposed the only reason they hadn't kicked her out was the fact that she kept a 3.7 grade point average. In desperation she had declared for art history this fall and quickly discovered it was as big a mistake as philosophy had been.

"Go to the dean. Maybe he'll make an exception or something."

"I did. Last week. He wouldn't." She had told the dean that it seemed to her that someone who had enough hours for a Ph.D. ought to be able to get a lousy bachelor's degree. The dean had smiled—very insincerely she thought—and said, "It helps if you have more than two courses in one field, Ms. Cunningham." Kristy was sure the dean was a Capricorn.

"So quit," Penny said and rolled over on her stomach.

"I can't. We're talking principle here." She had tried engineering, food science, home ec., social welfare, journalism and a few other majors, only to find her interest waning after a course or two. "Oh, Penny, I want something I can devote my life to. Something that makes my heart beat faster just thinking about it."

"How about becoming a missionary?"

"They don't offer a degree in missionary. Just like they don't offer one in astrology, which I think is very short-sighted of them. I could whip through twenty-four credits of astrology in no time." She lay the art history book aside and picked up Penny's astrological chart. "Did you realize you're probably in for a great adventure next month? The sun will be in the sign of Libra, Jupiter eclipsed by the moon...hmmm...under the influence of Jupiter."

Penny grunted and muttered that she would rather be in an investment banking house under the influence of a bull market.

On a lark they had wandered into an astrologer's tent during Aquafest, Penny to find out whether she should continue dating MBAs or switch to pre-meds—her theory being that an MBA might not be able to handle the competition from a wife who made more money than he did— Kristy to find out what she wanted to be when she grew up.

She had carefully explained her dilemma to the woman astrologer, who smiled and nodded and patted her hand. "It's to be expected, my dear. You're a Gemini." Kristy smiled, even though Madame Violet made her sign sound like a disease. "Bright, energetic, scattered. Flighty at times. A split personality, my dear. You Geminis get bored with things." She patted Kristy's hand again. "One day you will find the challenge you need." She had leaned close and wagged a ring-heavy finger in Kristy's face. "Never marry a Virgo."

The astrologer's assessment of her life came as a great relief to Kristy. It swept away all the guilt she had felt about skipping around from one thing to another. She even began to dabble in astrological charts and found it fascinating. Just before tuition time, she made up charts and explained about Geminis to her mother. Her mother said she was looking to rationalize her flightiness, which was totally unnecessary as she had been flighty since age two—inherited from her father's side of the family, no doubt—and it was all just as well since in her experience flighty women always married well. Kristy knew this was a jab at her grandfather since her wonderful banker father was one of the most unflighty men in the entire world. She didn't mention astrology to her mother again.

Kristy sighed. "Well, all I can say is that art history is at least pretty and doesn't smell bad, which is more than I can say about some of my past majors."

"Banking, Kristy. Banking is where it's at," Penny said.

"Not according to my mother." But then her mother was more interested in husbands than degrees. She called weekly to check out Kristy's dating situation, ending each conversation with the usual admonition. "Remember, dear, no one in oil, real estate or banking. Stick with hotels, fast food and discount houses." Kristy bent over Penny's chart and was deep into moon phases and ruling planets when the phone rang.

The line was full of static when she answered.

"Miss Cunningham?"

"Speaking." It was probably a siding salesman.

"The Miss Cunningham who is the granddaughter of Virgil Cunningham?"

She sat up straighter. "Yes?"

"This is Samuel Eldridge in Mount Ida, Arkansas. Virgil's lawyer."

Kristy felt her heart beat a little faster. "Yes?" She had not seen her grandfather in years, but they had written to each other faithfully, ever since that last wonderful summer she'd spent in Mount Ida when she was twelve. She sometimes felt that Virgil Cunningham was the only person in the world who understood her. Of course, he, too, was a Gemini, which might explain why she was the only one in the family who understood *him*. She was working on his chart, too.

"Have you heard from Virgil lately?"

"No. I mean I haven't had a letter in a month or two." She felt her heart kick up another notch. "Has something happened?"

The lawyer cleared his throat. "Well, I don't know. I mean, well, Virgil's out of pocket and I thought maybe he'd gone off to visit you."

"Out of pocket? You mean he's missing?"

"I probably shouldn't have bothered you, Miss Cunningham, but Virgil and I always have coffee at the café on Saturday mornings, and he didn't show up last Saturday, which sometimes he doesn't, but he didn't show up yesterday either, and I've never known him to miss two Saturdays in a row. Nobody's seen him, and I *am* a bit worried."

Kristy thought the man sounded more than a bit worried. She took a deep breath and told herself to calm down. "How long has he been gone, Mr. Eldridge?"

"Well, it's hard to say. He's been quite beside himself about this new mine, comparing it to the McEarl mine, of all things. I don't suppose you would have occasion to know about it, but there is a lot of poaching and some *very* unseemly characters around here these days, and he usually tells somebody when he's going off, and he's been gone well over a week."

Kristy tried her best to follow the rambling account. Her grandfather had never said a word in his letters about any new mine, or about going off into the woods for long periods of time. She tried to remember what she knew about the McEarl mine, which was very little, except that some of the finest quartz crystal in the world came from that mine. Surely her grandfather would have told her. "You mean you think somebody..." She couldn't bring herself to say the words.

"I don't know what to think. Virgil and I go back a ways, and while he does tend to be secretive at times, I like to think Virgil confides in me on important matters. Michael's looking after the mine, although how he finds the time is beyond me what with his own mine to see to, and *he's* not a bit worried. He says Virgil's just off on one of his crystal hunts, and Michael's a fine boy, but these young folks don't tend to worry like they ought to about things. No offense, miss." His words faded away into static. "I'm calling everyone I can think of who might have seen Virgil and I don't care a bit if Michael thinks I'm a worrywart. I have tried to tell Virgil we are not getting any younger, not that he listens, of course, but in my opinion he is much too old to be wandering around these mountains alone."

Kristy had never imagined that there were people who spoke in paragraphs instead of sentences, but Mr. Eldridge managed it quite well. Michael who? Her grandfather had never mentioned any Michael working with him, and she didn't think of Virgil as old, and in his letters he was still sharp as a tack, but what if he *was* getting forgetful and had wandered off and fallen or... "I'll be there tonight, Mr. Eldridge."

"I didn't mean for you to drop everything and come over here, Miss Cunningham. Michael may be right." She could almost hear the man wipe his brow in relief. "It would be a comfort, though, if you were here."

"I'll be there tonight."

Kristy slammed down the phone. She called the art department and told the secretary that most of her family had been in a terrible car wreck and were not expected to live. She would be back when she could. She stuck her head out the patio doorway. "Penny, I'm going to Mount Ida. Tell Mom I'm taking part in a psychology department experiment on sensory deprivation and will be incommunicado for at least two weeks."

Penny turned to stare at her. "Mount Ida? It's a little early for skiing, isn't it?"

"Mount Ida's in Arkansas, Penny. It's Granddad. He's in trouble. On second thought, tell Mom it might be longer. I'll probably become deranged during the experiment and go directly to the asylum." Her mother would die if she knew her precious daughter was leaving school to look for the man she credited with not only ruining her marriage, but also trying his best to turn her daughter into a "rustic."

"Kristy," Penny wailed. "What about school?"

"This may be the big challenge Madame Violet predicted. I'll call you. I may need some financial advice."

She quickly changed from shorts to jeans and a cotton shirt, then threw a few things in a suitcase. Jeans for the mine, a tailored suit for the lawyer, and a sundress just in case. Her hair, long and for the most part unmanageable, was a mess, but there was no time to worry about it. The long pigtail made her look about twelve, but it went with the faded Levi's jeans and black T-shirts of the art department group. Worn loose her hair made her look older and more sophisticated, but it also made her look more like a city girl. It was a problem deciding, but she supposed she might have to look after the mine and things until she found her grandfather, and there was this tiresome Michael to deal with, so older was surely better. She undid the pigtail, applied gel, wielded a blow dryer and brush, and in the end jammed a straw hat on her head and tied a red silk scarf around it all.

She hauled everything outside, put the top down on the BMW, slathered her face and arms with sunscreen and headed for Arkansas.

KRISTY WAS NOT given to tears unless animals or small children were involved. She drove from Austin to Mount Ida dry-eyed and determined, lecturing herself all the way about family responsibilities and business management instead of allowing herself to think about all the awful things that might have happened to her grandfather. She didn't know the first thing about mining, but she knew about family responsibilities, and she would take care of her grandfather's mine and his rock shop and his house—and anything else that needed taking care of—as if they were her own until he got back. *Correct that,* she thought, *until I find him.* Finding her grandfather would be the first order of business.

Kristy was a great believer in hunches and feelings and such, and to her mind and according to the chart she had started on him last week, Virgil could not possibly be dead. He was simply...misplaced. Temporarily.

She pulled into her grandfather's driveway late in the afternoon, just as the sun began to drift down behind the pine trees. When she looked at the little frame house and the crooked sign that said, Rock Shop, her lips began to quiver. Nothing had changed since that summer she was twelve, the last summer she ever spent with her grandfather. A forty-nine Ford still sat on blocks beside the house, the front porch was still a collection of clutter, and the pole building by the road, with walls of peeled saplings and chicken wire, was still full of warped cardboard boxes and rocks and dusty crystals. She knew the wire-topped tables and the great rusty tanks where he cleaned the crystals would still be in the backyard.

Yet everything had changed. She had grown up, and her grandfather had grown old, and it might be too late to tell him how much she loved him. Sitting there in the quiet beginnings of evening, images of that last childhood summer came flooding back, and along with the memories came the tears.

They stopped just as quickly when a cold wet tongue snaked under her arm and up to lick her face. She jerked away and looked into a face so wrinkled and sad she didn't know whether to laugh or cry some more. It belonged to a huge black and tan hound who seemed determined to wash her tears away with the largest, wettest tongue she'd ever seen.

When she finally managed to fend off his attentions, he stood quietly, head and front legs still on the car, a worried look on his face. "You must be Mercury," she said. He smiled at the sound of his name and tried to lick her again. "Only Granddad would stick a name like that on somebody like you. In his letters he made you sound like some kind of great mythological creature." The dog shook his head enthusiastically as if denying all such claims. "He said he was training you to do all sorts of wonderful things." She rubbed his head with one hand and wiped her face with the other.

"Okay, Mercury, if you'll get down, I'll get out of the car." The dog wagged his whole body and looked worried but refused to move. "I guess 'get down' wasn't part of the training, huh?" Finally, Kristy scooted over to the passenger side and got out. The dog ambled around the car to meet her, wagging his body and smiling and rubbing on her like a cat. He was enormous. She patted his head and noted that he smelled faintly of something long dead, but at least he was company and she wouldn't have to go into the house by herself.

When she tried the front door, it was locked. Her surprise mingled with a touch of fear. Virgil, she recalled, kept a key under a broken chunk of milky white quartz that lay by the door, but she could never remember him locking the house. The chunk of quartz lay where it always had, and when she tipped it over, the key was there, dull and dusty, as if it had not been used in years.

A few minutes later she stood in the living room of the little house. Every flat surface bristled with quartz crystals—points and clusters in every conceivable size and shape, each one in some way different from all the others. The late-afternoon sun touched a row of exquisite points sitting in the west window and strewed soft, delicate rainbows across the dingy floor. The house spoke of an old man living alone, but the crystals sparkled as if they had been polished only moments ago. These were Virgil's favorites, and he could touch each one and tell you exactly where it came from and when he dug it. She supposed, with the current crystal craze, he was afraid someone would steal his treasures, and that explained the locked door. As she glanced around the room, she saw the picture she had sent him, a snapshot taken on Padre Island. In it she was all windblown and half-hidden under a floppy straw hat, but he had put the photograph in a brass frame and set it on his desk. It looked as polished as the crystals. The tears threatened to come back.

Suddenly Mercury raised his head and let out a mournful howl then thundered out of the house, the screen door slamming behind him. Kristy imagined him loping across the yard after a rabbit. She picked up a beautiful eight-inch crystal point, as clear as water, and held it up to the waning light.

The screen door slammed again, and she whirled around at the sound. A man stood by the front door, hidden in shadows. "Oh. If you're looking for crystals, I'm afraid we're closed. I mean, I just got here and, well, you see..." The man didn't move. It occurred to Kristy that he might be a burglar instead of a customer, except she didn't think they had burglars in Mount Ida. Perhaps it was some crazed crystal person searching for...whatever they searched for. Mercury had returned and was lumbering back and forth between them as if only he understood they both belonged there.

"Who are you?" the man asked in a harsh voice as he stepped into the dying light.

CHAPTER TWO

KRISTY QUICKLY reached over and turned on a lamp. A man of clay towered over her by a foot. Patches of faded denim, white T-shirt and sun-bleached hair peeked out of the coating of dried, red clay. And startling, blue-gray eyes. Eyes that held her, perhaps because they were so striking, or perhaps because they were the only part of him that seemed alive. It was rather like looking at some lovely, ancient statue come to life. "I could ask you the same thing," she murmured and wished she had said it with more authority.

"I belong here. You don't. Haven't you people ever heard of private property? Out." He waved toward the door.

She didn't have the foggiest idea what he was talking about, but the hard edge in his voice not only broke the spell of his eyes, it sent her blood pressure up several points. "I'm Kristy Cunningham. This is my grandfather's house. Who the blazes are you?" Judging from his appearance, he probably worked in Virgil's mine.

He stared at her. "What are *you* doing here?"

She was pleased with the confusion in his voice, but she had a feeling it was temporary. "If you've come by to check on things, I appreciate it, but it won't be necessary." She wasn't here to pass the time of day with some man who wouldn't know the first thing about Virgil's business, let alone his whereabouts. "You *do* work for my grandfather, don't you?" She put the crystal back on the windowsill, then turned to face him, carefully avoiding the pull of his eyes, wondering instead how she could tactfully get rid of him and get on with the business at hand.

He walked closer. "I guess you could say that." He pushed her straw hat back and touched her hair. "You looked better in pigtails."

Kristy stepped back, away from the warm and earthy smell of his hand. "How would you know what I looked like in pigtails?"

"I'm Mike Ferguson. I came by to feed Merc and visit with him for a while." He ran his hand through his hair, and bits of clay flew out. "I thought you were a crystal freak."

Kristy searched her mind for the name. Michael, as in looking after things. Ferguson, as in—"You're, you're Mikey! Chester's—"

He nodded. "Right. Chester's grandson, but it's Mike now. I repeat, what in heaven's name are you doing here?"

Kristy smiled with relief. Chester and Virgil had been cronies for as long as anyone could remember. "Oh, thank goodness. Have you found him yet?" It was only after she blurted out the question that she remembered this was also the Michael who thought Mr. Eldridge was a worrywart and who was not worried one bit about Virgil.

A frown cracked the clay on his forehead. "Who?"

"Granddad." She had the sinking feeling that Mr. Eldridge hadn't bothered to tell Mike about his inquiries.

He shook his head. "I don't have the slightest idea what you're talking about."

"Mr. Eldridge called." She took a deep breath, feeling as if there wasn't quite enough air to breathe. "This morning. Oh, never mind. He told me how you felt about the whole thing. I just hope Grandad's not dead in the woods someplace."

His frown deepened, and more clay cracked. "Dead? Virgil? Is that what Sam told you?"

She had a moment of doubt about just what the lawyer *had* said. "Well, not exactly, but more or less. But I would know if he were dead. I started his chart last week, and he was entering a period of unparalleled prosperity. They probably beat him up and left him for dead and he's in a hospital somewhere with amnesia." When she said it out loud, she realized how melodramatic the idea sounded, even to her. But it was too late to back down. "I can't understand why you're not worried."

He rubbed the back of his neck as if he had a sudden headache. "Chart. Right. I suppose you're into crystals, too? May the Lord preserve me from young women who are *into* anything." Before she could answer, he held up his hand. "Never mind. So Sam told you to drop everything and sail over here because Virgil had been whisked away or some such. Did he by any chance have a clue as to the identity of these kidnappers or whatever they're supposed to be?"

"Well, not exactly, but he did mention poachers and unseemly characters. And he didn't ask me to come, but—" He was making fun of her. She couldn't believe any grandson of Chester's could be so flippant about things.

"Well, you wasted a trip. Damn Sam, anyway. He's a worrywart at best, but this approaches Chicken Little and the sky is falling," he said.

Kristy wasn't sure what to say to that, so she fanned herself with her hat and asked him how long her grandfather had been gone.

He shook his head. "Maybe a week."

"It's longer than a week. He's missed two Saturdays at the café with Mr. Eldridge."

He stopped rubbing his neck. "Wait a minute. You're over here because Virgil missed two gossip sessions with Sam? I don't believe it." She heard the incredulity in his voice. "Look, Virgil disappears sometimes. I never ask where to, because it's none of my business. You made a long trip for nothing."

She fanned herself faster. "Nothing? You call my grandfather being missing, nothing?"

He leaned against the chair, arms crossed over his chest. Although she couldn't be sure through all that clay, she thought the vein in his forehead was pulsing, but his voice was as calm and cool as ice. "He is not missing."

The irritating calm of his voice and posture had just the opposite effect on Kristy. She felt her temper begin to rise. "Well, he certainly is not here, and obviously hasn't been here for some time. Are you telling me you know where he is?"

"No. As a matter of fact I don't."

Her blood pressure went up another notch. "You don't know where he is, Mr. Eldridge doesn't know where he is, nobody's seen him, but he isn't missing. Right?"

"That's right."

"You have a very peculiar way of looking at things. Have you even looked for him?"

Anger blazed in his eyes for a brief second. "No, I have not looked for him. *If* I did, and *if* I happened to find him, he would be mightily insulted, and *I* would be mightily embarrassed. He'll be back. He always comes back, Kristy.''

''But what if he doesn't?'' she wailed.

He slapped the back of a chair and looked at the ceiling. ''I don't believe this. If you knew anything about Virgil, you would know he just...goes off sometimes.''

''I happen to know a great deal about my grandfather,'' she snapped with a confidence she didn't feel. Maybe she didn't know Virgil as well as she thought she did. They'd been apart a long time. ''Goes off where?''

''I don't know where. Off in the woods. Off looking for crystals. Off bird-watching for all I know. It's what Virgil does. He's done it for years.'' His voice filled the room. ''But of course you wouldn't know that, would you?''

The air crackled with tension and implication. ''Well, I think that's a cavalier attitude. Mr. Eldridge thinks he's missing and that there may be foul play.''

''Sam must not have enough work to keep him busy. Believe me, Virgil is not missing and there has been no foul play. And if you will excuse me, Mercury is starving.'' He turned away from her and went into the kitchen. She followed, her rescue mission in serious doubt now.

''You really think he's just off in the woods?''

''Yes, Kristy, that is what I really think. He'll be back in a day or two, just like he always is.'' She watched him pour dog food into a pan and add water. Mercury stood watching, his tail thumping against the cabinets. Mike put the pan down and bent over the sink. ''We hit a little underground spring today,'' he said, as if to explain the clay. His voice was muffled by the sounds of running water and Mercury's enthusiastic eating.

Kristy watched him soap his face and arms and tried not to watch the muscles in his back work against the only part of the T-shirt that was clay free. As he let the water run over his head, it occurred to Kristy that this man was a far cry from the wiry teenaged boy she remembered. He was lean and hard and full of muscles and...and...and she needed to get her mind back to her business. If at this point there was any business to put her mind to. He seemed so sure about Virgil, and his arguments were convincing.

He finally stood up and swiped at his face and arms with a towel. His face, even when covered with several days' stubble of beard, was a study in angles and planes, with high cheekbones and sharply defined jaw. Kristy thought his eyes looked more blue than gray now that his skin was a dark, bronzy brown instead of clay-red. She also thought it was awfully hot in the tiny kitchen. She picked at the brim of her hat while he leaned against the cabinets and looked at her. From head to toe.

"Well, you look a little different from the pigtailed brat I remember, but you didn't grow out of being a busybody, did you?"

Kristy flinched, but she was determined to get along with this man, since he seemed to think he was "in charge" of things in Virgil's absence. Perhaps if they talked about those long-ago summers, he would quit frowning. "Brat? I wasn't a brat. *You* were a bully, as I remember it." She rearranged the salt and pepper shakers on the table. "It was that last summer I remember the best. Chester took me fishing. And you took me for a ride on your motorcycle. My mother almost died when she found out." Kristy could remember little of the ride except clinging to a wiry boy and flying along the country roads as if they might take off at any moment and soar over the treetops. "I'm really sorry about Chester. Granddad wrote me when your grandfather died. He still misses him," she said softly.

"Yeah, so do I." He toweled his hair. "You never came back after that summer."

His words hung in the quiet air like an accusation. "Mom and Dad divorced the next year. Mom wouldn't let me, and Dad went off to Atlanta and— You never came back to see me after the motorcycle ride." He didn't respond. The more she remembered about that summer, the more she remembered how much she had despised Mike Ferguson. Despised him as only a twelve-year-old girl can despise an older boy. It made her smile. "So how's the mine coming?" she asked as if she knew all there was to know about it.

He shrugged and watched Mercury consume the last of his food. "Fine." Drops of water glistened in the dark-blond stubble on his face.

He hung the towel on a hook, then walked past her. At the door he turned and gave her a ghost of a smile. She could only imagine how dazzling his *real* smile would be. "It's been nice seeing you again. I'll tell Virgil you came by when I see him." He rubbed the stubble on his cheek with his knuckles as if trying to think of something else to say. "If you'll leave your number by the phone, I'll call you in the unlikely event Virgil doesn't turn up." He opened the door and stepped onto the porch.

She trailed after him. "Wait a minute. I'm not going anywhere. I'm sure there's plenty of work to do around here, with the mine and all. And there's Granddad to find and..." She could see the long, sinewy muscles of his back tighten against his T-shirt before he turned to face her. There was something new in his expression, and she didn't think she was going to like it.

"You're what?"

Kristy noticed that his voice was even less friendly than it had been, but she caught her breath and stared right back at him. Right into those flashing blue eyes. "I mean it's been awfully nice of you to fill in, but I'm sure you have other things to do." Her heart was thumping at an alarming rate, but she had no intention of letting Mike Ferguson bully her around now.

A muscle twitched in his jaw, but he took a deep breath and expelled it before he spoke. "Fill in? Kristy, dear, I *own* part of this mine, and I don't need any help with it."

She swallowed hard. Her grandfather had never said one word in his letters about Mike Ferguson, let alone about his owning anything. He *had* talked about "the boy" helping him, but . . . surely Mike Ferguson wasn't "the boy." She experienced a sudden sinking feeling as she realized that he was. "Oh . . . Mr. Eldridge said you have your own mine."

"I do. I also have a piece of this one. What did you think? That I was just hired help?"

"Well, no, but Mr. Eldridge didn't mention a partner, and I thought—"

"The mine is between Virgil and me. It's not Sam's business, and it's not yours. I'll have Virgil call you the minute he gets back."

He was going to send her home. An image of the art history book floated across her mind's eye, and his dismissive tone seemed to fly all over her. Actually, everything about him flew all over her. She sucked in a breath of the cool evening air. "Well, I think Granddad would want me to stay."

"How could you *possibly* know what your grandfather would want. You haven't seen him in, what, ten, twelve years?" He waved a hand at the house. "I guess you can stay the night, but I'm taking care of the place, and I don't want anything else to take care of."

The anger and hostility in his voice stung Kristy, and she couldn't begin to imagine the why of it. "I am perfectly capable of taking care of myself and the place."

"The well is unreliable. It won't stand two-hour showers."

"I don't take two-hour showers, and if I recall, all you have to do is prime that well occasionally." She was surprised that the memory of how to handle the well came back so easily.

"I thought you were in school or something." He ran his fingers through his hair and drops of water flew. A few moments ago, it would have distracted her, but now she was too upset by his words.

She sensed he was trying to control his anger. "I was, but this is more important."

He gave her that ghosty smile again, but it didn't begin to reach the coldness in his eyes. "Kristy, I don't need any help with the mine. I know about mines. And Virgil doesn't need finding. And Sam needs a good kick in the rear for starting all this. If he weren't so old, I might just do it."

She crossed her arms and glared at him. "I'm staying. It would be foolish to drive all the way here, then not stay to see Granddad, and since you're so sure he'll be back any minute, well, it will only be a brief stay."

He threw his head back and looked at the darkening sky. "Why me, Lord?" His fingers tapped a staccato on the porch rail as he leveled his eyes to hers once more. "You know, you haven't changed a bit. You're still as stubborn as a mule. I have no idea when Virgil will be back. It might be a month."

"You just said a day or two."

"It might be longer this time."

"So I'll stay however long it is. But I plan to find him long before any month is out." She had no idea why Mike Ferguson was so anxious to get rid of her, but she was tired of his lame excuses. "He might be upset if you ferret him out of the woods, but I don't think he'll be the least upset if I go looking for him." She could almost see the blood pounding in the veins of his forehead and knew she'd hit a sensitive spot. It dawned on her suddenly that he wanted her gone so she *wouldn't* see her grandfather. She had to wonder why.

"Fine. I can't throw you out, I suppose." He poked a finger at her nose. "Just stay out of my way and out of Virgil's business. I'm sure while you're here you'll want to clean the house from stem to stern, which Virgil will hate, but you can explain it to him if you're still here when he gets back."

Kristy clenched her fists at her sides and took several deep breaths. "I had more in mind than house drudge." She watched as his gaze moved from her eyes to somewhere in the middle of her shirt. "I want to see the mine."

"The mine is my territory. It's no place for a—"

"Girl? Is that what you were going to say?"

He looked at her for a long moment. "I was going to say woman. At least part of you has grown up."

"Maybe you could keep me away when I was a kid, but you can't keep me away now, *Mikey*." Let him put *that* in his pipe and smoke it. As he stalked angrily to the truck, she couldn't help but notice that he moved with the grace of an animal—even when he was stalking. Angrily.

"We'll see, Kristy."

"You must be a Virgo—" she called. "And if you think I came here to clean house, you've got another think coming."

She stood and stared after the truck. She was going to find her grandfather whether he wanted to be found or not. If Mike Ferguson was as important as he seemed to think, Virgil would have called him something besides "the boy" in his letters. He would have told her Mike was a partner. Virgil told her everything.

When she stormed back into the house, Mercury jumped up, wrapped his front legs over her shoulders and licked her face. "Down, boy. Sit. Lie down. Go *away!*" That seemed to do the trick. She mopped the slobber off her face, then turned on every light and began to clean. It had nothing to do with Mike Ferguson. It was simply what the women in her family did when they were mad. Mercury climbed into the old overstuffed sofa and looked worried. She swept and scrubbed and dusted and talked non-stop to the dog, who finally closed his eyes but still looked worried. "You do dead dog real well, Merc, and you should look worried. You're going to get a bath tomorrow." She would also go through the desk to see if she could find any clue to where Virgil might have gone.

When things were clean to suit her, she called her father. She would wait to call her mother. Perhaps send a note saying she was in a private asylum as a result of the experiment. "Daddy?" She put on her best voice.

"Hi, baby, how are you?"

"Fine. How was the banking thing in London?"

"Boring. Did you call to tell me your new major for this semester?"

"Daddy, don't be tacky. It's art history."

He laughed. "Sounds like a winner. Just the other day I heard some guys at the club talking about the shortage of art historians."

Kristy laughed. Her father didn't take her degree changes too seriously. "Daddy, Granddad may be missing." There was a long silence. "Daddy?"

"Yes, honey. *May* be missing? What does that mean?" She repeated what she knew and what Mike had said. "Well, Mike is probably right. Virgil has a long history of disappearing," he said quietly.

"Daddy, he's your father."

He sighed. "I know that, Kristy, but I'm not sure *he* always remembers it."

Kristy was quiet for what seemed like a long time. Her father had always refused to talk about the rift with his father, but she thought it had to do with his becoming an investment banker, and something to do with her mother. She didn't think there had been any communication between her father and grandfather since her parents' divorce. And there certainly hadn't been much before. "Daddy, I'm here in Mount Ida. Helping out."

Her father sighed. "He always was determined to get somebody in the family involved in his dreams and his rocks. Honey, go back to school. He's off looking for another rainbow and a pot of gold. He'll be back."

"He is not, and I can't."

"Kristy, honey, your grandfather was always a dreamer. He's like the old prospectors, always looking for the big one." His voice softened. "His mines never quite turn out that way."

Kristy felt the tears sting her eyes. "But this one might, Daddy. I want to help."

"Kristy, baby, you don't even know Virgil." When she didn't respond, his voice changed. "Okay, let me know what happens. I'll come if you need me."

"Thanks Daddy. You're a peach."

"No I'm not. I'm a sucker for my little girl. But don't let him hurt you with his dreams, baby. Just don't let him do it."

Kristy replaced the receiver and went to the car to get her suitcase. Tomorrow would be a busy day. She would see Mr. Eldridge first thing, then tour the mine and get Mike Ferguson straightened out. Just the thought of that encounter caused her stomach to tighten. Why did all the really gorgeous men have to be such jerks?

She ate some peanut butter and crackers, took a long bath and finally lay down on the sagging bed with *Quartz Crystal Deposits of Western Arkansas, Geological Survey Bulletin No. 973-E.* When she tried to read what appeared to be the finest print she had ever seen, the tears came again. She *had* meant to come see her grandfather every summer, but after her parents' divorce the summers came and went and she wrote her letters and stayed away. In some way, she supposed she'd been afraid to come. Afraid the reality would be different from the wonderful summers she remembered, summers with Virgil and Chester doting on her, entertaining her, turning her vacations into one long treasure hunt. From the time she could remember, hardly a civil word had passed between her father and Virgil, yet her father had wanted her to spend time with the old man, as if she were part of a debt he couldn't pay himself. But she'd never questioned it, lest the summers come to an end.

That last summer, she had returned to Dallas sun-burned and peeling, scratched and scabbed, stained by the tenacious red clay of the area and blistered with poison ivy. Her mother had been appalled and forbade her to ever visit "that old reprobate" again. By the next year, her parents were divorced and she spent that summer in Atlanta with her father instead of Mount Ida with Virgil.

Kristy had been crushed when she realized she could spend time with her father or her grandfather, but not both. So she wrote to Virgil. Long letters filled with all her childish hopes and dreams, then letters filled with all her college disasters. He wrote back, long letters full of crystals, new mines and changing seasons. He had never asked her to come, as if he, too, were afraid things would be different.

And now she might never see him again, in spite of all Mike's assurances. Even that possibility made her all the more determined to look after his things until he got back, maybe even stay on and help for a while after that. She had a feeling about this new mine. A feeling that it would be all the things her grandfather had ever searched for. And Mike Ferguson would learn that Geminis—once they set their mind to something—were not to be trifled with. Even if the one doing the trifling had the nicest blue eyes in the world.

She stared at the fine print of the government publication, but her eyes fluttered shut, those blue eyes and sun-bleached hair replacing the fine print in her mind's eye.

Sometime in the night, Mercury scratched on the door and without really ever waking up, she let him out.

CHAPTER THREE

KRISTY WOKE early and, after drinking a cup of the worst instant coffee she had ever tasted, put on her tailored suit and fixed her hair and face to look as mature and businesslike as possible. She rummaged around Virgil's desk but found nothing which might indicate where he had gone.

When she went out to the car, Mercury was waiting in the back seat, smiling and wagging his body wildly. She rubbed his head and caught a whiff of something, the identity of which she did not even want to think about. "If you're going to ride in my car, Merc, old boy, you're going to have to quit consorting with whatever it is you consort with." She started to make him get out, but he looked so pitiful she finally relented.

By the time she got to Mount Ida, she had liberal amounts of dog slobber on the front of her suit and had to leave her jacket in the car.

Somehow, the old stone courthouse and square looked smaller than she remembered, and more of the buildings were vacant, yet there was an air of busy activity, with cars and trucks and people going about their business. She parked the car and told Mercury to stay. "You might also try slobbering on the outside of the car," she said, shaking a finger at him. He looked crushed but didn't move. "Stay and dead dog. Great repertoire, Merc."

She found Mr. Eldridge in his office above a hardware and home improvement store called The Corner. He bustled out from behind his desk as soon as she introduced herself. "Oh, Miss Cunningham, I am so glad to see you. You won't remember me, of course, but I remember Virgil bringing you to town all those years ago. Quite fond of cinnamon rolls, I remember."

A sudden memory of Sunday mornings and warm, yeasty rolls drowning in cinnamon and butter washed over Kristy as she shook the lawyer's hand.

"You were the most beautiful child. Not, of course, that you aren't now. I mean, you're even more lovely. Sometimes beautiful children don't turn out well, you know."

"Thank you. Actually, I believe I do remember you, Mr. Eldridge." Samuel Eldridge was an elderly gentleman who looked more like an absent-minded professor than a small-town lawyer, and she supposed most of his work was with deeds and wills, rather than such exotic things as murders and robberies. Stacks of dusty files covered his desk and most of the floor. The walls were crowded with plaques and framed testimonials to his community spirit. Kristy thought it all looked rather like a Mount Ida version of Dickens.

After exchanging pleasantries and abandoning her hope that he would offer her a cup of real coffee—which she would have killed for at the moment—she assumed what she hoped was a businesslike posture. "About my grandfather, Mr. Eldridge."

"Sam. You must call me Sam." He sat down behind the massive oak desk and leaned across toward her. "I want to be candid with you, Miss Cunningham, but I certainly do not wish to hurt your feelings when I tell you I do not approve of some of Virgil's financial dealings. Which, I might add, may have some bearing on his current situation.''

"Kristy." She smiled. "You can be perfectly candid with me, Mr. Eldridge. I know that my grandfather is kind of the black sheep of the family and that he has a tendency to see gold under every rainbow."

He relaxed. "Splendid."

He told her again to call him Sam, but she could no more call a man like him Sam than she could fly to the moon. Samuel, maybe. Sam, never. "Now, about—"

"Well, Virgil came to me at the beginning of summer and told me he'd found the mine to end all mines. I have always tried to advise Virgil in prudence in these matters, but it has been difficult at times. The next thing I knew he was working an old mine that has been abandoned for years. I believe Michael is helping him, both physically and financially."

Kristy smiled at his curious mixture of quaintness and legalese. "It's strange he never wrote me about it."

He put a finger to his lips. "Oh, my dear, it was a secret."

"And?" she said to encourage him.

He glanced around the room as if there might be spies hiding in the corner, then leaned even closer. "Well, this crystal thing has turned this part of the country into...well...crazy, that's what. Why, there are grown men, men who have been steady all their lives, just suddenly closing up their businesses and rushing off to dig crystals."

Kristy laughed. "That's because all us crazies in the cities are paying outrageous prices for your crystals."

"And," he whispered, "there are some very unsuitable people coming into the area."

Kristy assured him that she understood perfectly, although she had no idea what all this had to do with Virgil being missing.

"I knew you would. Well, the most curious thing is that after starting up this old mine, Virgil began to go off again, and he started to file bids on new mining sites. I prepare some of his bids, you know. I told him, finally, that I thought he should settle down and work the one mine and quit looking for any more of his 'big' ones. He was quite put out with me and said the day would come when I would eat those words. Of course, he wouldn't explain what he meant."

Kristy was beginning to think she had wandered into never-never land. "Yes, well, how do you think this all relates to his going off this time?"

Mr. Eldridge smiled. "Poaching, my dear. I think the old mine he and Michael are working is a sham, and that Virgil has bigger fish to fry."

Bigger fish. Right. "And?" She felt as if she would grow old and gray before she ever got the whole story out of Mr. Eldridge. If there *was* a story.

"Well, it's perfectly simple, Miss Kristy. Some of these unsuitable characters got wind of Virgil's *bigger fish* and followed him. I think Virgil is in grave danger. If not worse." He took off his wire-rim glasses and cleaned them. "I'm very glad you came, Miss Kristy. I've been worried sick."

Kristy felt a rush of affection for the old man. She wasn't at all sure his theory would hold water, but she was touched by his obvious concern for Virgil. "I plan to start looking for him today, Mr. Eldridge." She reached out and patted his hand. "Don't you worry. We'll find Granddad. I think maybe Mike knows where he went."

"Oh, dear, Michael must be quite put out with me for calling you."

Kristy thought that might be the understatement of the century, but she was not about to upset Mr. Eldridge any further. "Not at all. He understands perfectly."

"Virgil sat right in that chair, not a month ago, and told me he couldn't wait to tell you about everything, but he said he wouldn't do it until he had something to show you."

"He wanted me to come back? To see something?"

"Oh, my, yes. Virgil always knew you would come back."

Her lip quivered. He wanted her to come but thought somehow he had to have something special for her. She almost cried over the wasted years, the years when neither of them knew how to say what they felt. "He did?"

"Of course, my dear. Shortly after your eighteenth birthday, Virgil came to me and insisted that I make out a power of attorney and a will. Both in your favor."

Kristy felt the tears well up. "He never told me."

"No. He said if anything happened to him, sickness or death, you were the one he trusted to do the right thing. For him, and for his crystals." He brightened. "So, in Virgil's absence, I suppose you have the power to take care of his business."

"I guess I do. I'm going to help with the mine."

"Oh dear, have you discussed this with Michael?"

She stood up and smiled reassuringly. "Yes indeed. He can hardly wait."

"Splendid. Let me know if you need anything while you're here. Michael is a fine boy, but he tends to be a bit headstrong at times."

Kristy smiled. "I did get that impression. He seems almost . . . protective of Granddad."

"Indeed. He's been like a son to Virgil."

"Really?" Just what she needed, a saint and a surrogate son—and a gorgeous one at that—running the mine entrusted to her. "Well, I'm sure it will all work out, Mr. Eldridge."

The lawyer shuffled papers and looked uncomfortable. "Uh, were you actually planning to go to the mine and work? I mean—" He made motions with his hands.

"Do you think Mr. Ferguson might not like that?"

He tried to smile but didn't quite manage it. "Splendid boy, Mike. I'm so glad you've come. You will let me know the minute you hear anything."

"The very minute, Mr. Eldridge." She said her goodbyes and left, feeling rather deflated about the morning. As much as she hated to admit it, Mike's theory about Virgil sounded a good deal more plausible than Mr. Eldridge's. She wondered if the sweet old lawyer had all his oars in the water. All of which left her with the problem of what to do. She supposed she should go to the mine and apologize to Mike for her hysteria of the night before, although the prospect was not appealing. He would no doubt act smug and superior and help her pack her bags for home. On the other hand, suppose Mr. Eldridge was right but just a little fluffy in his tale-telling, like Miss Marple. After all, there was little doubt that Mike wanted her out of "Dodge," pronto, and she couldn't think of any reason for that—unless he had something to hide in his dealings with Virgil. As she walked around the little square in search of a cup of coffee—which seemed to be as scarce in Mount Ida as at the house—she decided she wasn't going anywhere until she saw her grandfather and made sure everything was on the up and up with his new business venture, and took a closer look at Mike's motives for being so protective of Virgil.

She got in the car, fending off Mercury's attentions, then got back out when she realized she didn't have the slightest idea where the mine was. She went back to Mr. Eldridge and came out again with vague directions and an extensive explanation of how long it had been since he'd been out that way. She stopped by the store to pick up a few necessities, including ground coffee, then by the house to change into jeans. She stuck a small note-pad and pencil in her pocket, just in case she ran across any clues to Virgil's whereabouts, then headed north. Mercury was by now firmly ensconced in the front seat.

She left the highway a mile from her grandfather's place and took a road that wound through a little valley bright with late-summer sun. When she came to the fork in the road, she turned right at the ramshackle barn Mr. Eldridge had mentioned and found herself on a rutted track, going almost straight up a mountainside. The little car bucked and rocked from side to side and Kristy began to worry that dear Mr. Eldridge had probably *never* been "out this way." Mercury licked her ear and howled and hung his head over the side of the car, in spite of all her pleas for him to play dead dog.

When she came to a gate, she stopped. Although the metal looked old and rusty, the No Trespassing sign was new and bright. She hesitated, then got out of the car and opened the gate. A weathered board lay in the weeds beside the gate post with faded letters on it. Cunningham Mine. It had hung on the front porch of her granddad's house years ago. She picked it up and looked for some way to hang it, but the wire attachments had rusted away long ago. She found a pink silk scarf in the glove compartment and tied the sign to the gate. When it was hanging straight and proud enough to suit her, she got in the car and drove through the entry to the lane.

She was almost at the top of the hill when a rabbit raced out of the weeds and onto the road. Unfortunately, Mercury saw it and bounded across her and out of the car. Somehow while she was buried momentarily under the monstrous dog, the steering wheel got away from her and when the dust cleared, the car sat at a peculiar slant, one wheel in the ditch.

She tried reverse. Nothing happened. She got out of the car, ready to do great bodily harm to the dog, but he had abandoned his chase and just sat in the middle of the road, tail wagging, a worried look on his face. She shook a finger at him, began a stern lecture and ended up laughing. "Oh, Merc, Daddy would die if he knew what we'd done to his Christmas present to me."

Kristy decided her best course was simply to wait, that someone would eventually come by, if this was the right mine and if they were working it today. So she sat on the hood of the car and took a good look at the countryside. The mountains around her were cloaked in pines and hardwoods, and in a month or so, autumn would turn the hillsides into a patchwork of brilliant reds and yellows against the dark green pines. She knew it would be spectacular and hoped she would still be around to see it. To the west, she saw evidence of the clear-cutting that her grandfather got so worked up about in his letters. The hillside lay brown and naked in the bright sun, as if some great machine had crawled across it and eaten everything in its path.

In a few minutes, she heard, then saw, the pickup come flying down the mountain followed by a rooster tail of dust. When the truck stopped beside her and the dust began to settle, she saw with dismay that the driver was Mike Ferguson. She waited beside her car.

"Hi." She gave him a small wave and noticed that he was not covered with clay this morning. His face was clean shaven and a lovely dark bronze above his faded chambray work shirt. A John Deere cap shaded his eyes, but she knew they would be the blue of the open sea in the bright sunlight. She also knew they would telegraph either anger or laughter over her mishap.

He leaned out of the truck and looked at the car, then at her. "I would have thought it almost impossible to drive off the road in broad daylight."

She pulled her own hat lower on her head. "Actually, it was Mercury's fault. He saw this rabbit, and—"

Mike got out of the truck and slammed the door. "And went right over you and out of the car. Right?" He pushed his cap back, and she realized she had been all too right about his eyes—at least about the color. His expression was unreadable.

"Right." She bent down and patted the dog to keep from staring at the hard ridges of muscle under the thin cotton shirt. She felt a bit dizzy…from the hot sun, no doubt.

The dog ran to Mike and began to rub against him. Mike ruffled his ears. "Merc is a very unreliable passenger." He walked around and looked at the car. "What are you doing up here?"

"I was coming to see the mine. And talk to you. About last night." Why did she feel so uncomfortable with him?

"See the mine? I supposed you had come out to take it over." He leaned against the truck and crossed his arms. "A little supervising to start the day?"

She ignored his sarcasm, determined to start out on the right foot this morning. "I had nothing of the sort in mind. I would just like to see it." She cleared her throat and tried again, conjuring up an image of Penny discussing high finance—she would be calm and cool. "I went to see Mr. Eldridge this morning."

He nodded and gave her a serious look. "Good move, Kristy. Did your morning horoscope tell you to take care of legal matters today?" He opened the tailgate of the truck and the dog sailed in.

Kristy curbed her growing anger. "Look, I came here to see the mine and to try to have a civilized conversation with you. I guess we can forget the latter, so let's move on to the mine."

"I don't have time this morning. I have to go to town and get some bearings. One of the machines is down."

"Fine. You go to town, I'll go to the mine." She pulled her hat down and started up the hill. He caught her before she'd gone a hundred feet.

"What about last night?"

"Nothing."

He pushed her hat back and covered her forehead with his hand. "I think you've been in the sun too long. Now what did you want to talk about?"

His hand was calloused and hard and cool and gentle and . . . her face was burning up. She batted his hand away. "I was a little hysterical last night. I went to see Mr. Eldridge this morning, and I guess maybe you're more right about Granddad than he is." She could sense some of the tension fall away from him. "I mean, Mr.

Eldridge is a dear man, but he does seem to have a flair for the dramatic.''

"Well, I'm glad you've come to your senses."

"I'm not saying I totally accept your version, but I'm willing to wait awhile and see."

"Great. I'll get your car out. I'm sure you're anxious to get back to school."

She took a deep breath and tried to control her growing anger. "I said wait, Mike. That means here. In Mount Ida."

He took off the cap and slapped it against his leg, again and again. "Why didn't I know that?"

"Why are you so anxious to get rid of me?"

"Because I don't want Virgil upset."

"Upset? You think *I* would upset Granddad?"

He put the cap back on. "Yeah. That's what I think."

"Why?" When he didn't answer, she tried again. "And I'm just supposed to take it on blind faith that you know what's best for Granddad."

"You got it." He kicked a rock off the road and into the ditch. "I suppose if I don't show you the mine, you'll go anyway."

She smiled through clenched teeth. She wanted answers, but she knew she wouldn't get anything more from him. She would try to figure out his motives later, when she could think it through without distractions. "You suppose right."

"And no doubt kill yourself or distract the men or figure out some other way to cost me a day's work. Come on."

She swept past him and climbed into the truck. The truck cab seemed awfully small, and she felt as if she were about twelve again. And it was all his fault. She hadn't felt twelve since she was at least fifteen.

"You *have* seen a mining operation, haven't you?"

"Of course I've seen a mining operation."

CHAPTER FOUR

WHEN THEY TOPPED the hill, Kristy was totally unprepared for what lay in front of her. The top of the mountain had been skimmed off and replaced by enormous piles of clay and slag. Giant bulldozers and other earth-moving equipment rumbled out of a hole in the ground that looked as if one could bury a five-story building in it. It looked like pictures she had seen of strip mines out west, with roads snaking along stairstepped sides and around other dirt piles at the bottom. It was only when she saw what looked like a miniature pickup and toy men at the far end of the pit that she realized just how big the mine was. Dust fogged everywhere.

It was not even close to what she remembered. Actually, she and Virgil had mostly dug holes in the ground in the national forest. He'd always seemed to be between mines in the summers, always looking for the big one.

Mike got out of the truck and motioned for her to follow him. He stopped beside a monstrous yellow machine. Kristy noted with a sinking feeling that the tires were about twice as tall as she was. "We'll ride down," he yelled over the sound of a dozer rumbling nearby. When she didn't move, he took her by the arm and led her toward the machine. "It's called a track loader."

"Right." She smiled and wondered how one got up to the seat, which looked about the same height as the terrace of her second-story apartment. Mike laced his fingers together and looked at her expectantly, then bent a little lower so she could easily put a foot in his cupped hands. Except she still didn't see any way to get to the first step without practically climbing him. It occurred to her that he might catapult her right over the machine.

"Do you want to see the mine or don't you?" he asked.

"Yes. I was just admiring the machine." She put her hand on his shoulder and stepped into his hands. He lifted her as if she were a feather. The movement was so swift, she grabbed at his hair to steady herself and her head swam, although she still wasn't more than six feet off the ground. When she felt his hand on the seat of her jeans, she grabbed at the metal rungs—they were obviously spaced for giants—and scrambled up, knowing he was right behind her. Inside the cab she wrapped her arm around a giant roll bar and refused to look at him.

"Hang on," he said, as he started the machine. Mercury ran along the edge of the pit and barked, but refused to follow them.

The great machine started down a steep incline carved out of the side of the pit, but Kristy's stomach seemed determined to stay at the top. She closed her eyes. "What keeps this thing from falling on its nose?" she yelled.

He leaned close and shouted in her ear. "Center of gravity. And track loaders don't have noses."

"How nice." Her cheek and ear burned where his warm breath touched her, and she knew darn well he was enjoying her reaction to all this, and she despised him every bit as much as she had when she was twelve years old. Maybe more. She had to hang on to keep from getting bounced out.

Then they were at the bottom of the pit, and he was on the ground helping her down. Somehow, his hands were on her waist, lifting her, swinging her, through the air. In her effort to get out of his grasp, she ended up more or less sliding down his front. It made her queasy stomach all the more queasy, and when she looked at him, that ghost of a smile played at his lips. She realized that he knew exactly what effect he had on her. She felt the blood rush to her face.

"I don't do this for all my foremen, you know."

"I do not want to be a foreman, I just want to look around." She shook off his hold, straightened her hat and her clothes and looked around. "Why didn't we drive down in the truck? Everybody else did." She pointed to the pickup that had looked so small from the top of the pit.

"Because the machine was up there, and it needed to come down here."

There were men scattered around the walls of the pit, digging with picks and other long tools. On her left, a wide vein of milky white quartz was visible. Two men squatted in a small cavelike opening in one wall, wrapping hunks of crystals in newspaper, then putting them in bushel baskets.

"I take it this was not the kind of mining you and Virgil did during your summer vacations?" His voice was light and mocking.

"Well, not exactly. But of course we were just . . . sampling different areas, looking for the right place. Have you hit the big one yet?"

"We're getting some nice rocks," he said in a non-committal voice.

"How long have you been here?" She had to yell over the noise of the equipment.

He leaned close. "A month."

She looked around in awe.

"It's an old mine. We've just worked it a little wider." He leaned even closer, and she felt his warm breath on her cheek. "But don't worry, it's only costing about ten thousand a month to dig. If you're so anxious to be involved, perhaps you'll contribute for a month or two."

"Ten thou—Oh!" Kristy swallowed hard. She was so overwhelmed by the whole thing she couldn't think of anything to say.

"But if we hit some good pockets, we'll get all that back and then some. The vein we're working has some pretty good industrial grade quartz. I'm sure you know all about white quartz for industrial and clear quartz for specimens."

"Of course."

He started toward a stack of baskets filled with what looked like lumps of clay and newspaper. "Don't wander off, and don't touch anything."

"Right." She glared defiantly at him, then marched off in the direction of the men and promptly fell into a sea of wet, gummy clay.

Mike rolled his eyes and offered his hand. "I believe I mentioned the underground spring? This is it. I believe I also told you not to wander off."

He practically had to drag her out of the mud. She had never encountered anything so sticky in all her life. As soon as she was free, she untangled herself from him and walked away again—on feet she was sure must weigh forty pounds apiece.

Catching up to her, he took her by the arm and led her toward an ancient truck. "Very hard on Reebok shoes. Not to mention designer jeans."

She refused to rise to the bait. She could almost hear him laughing himself silly. He stopped beside a large, orange Igloo water cooler and pulled a red bandanna from his hip pocket. Before she could protest, he had wet it, pushed her hat back and was wiping the clay from her face. The water was cold and his touch was none too gentle, yet—she snatched the neckerchief from him and stepped away from the magic of his hands. "I am perfectly capable of cleaning my own face."

"Oh, I'm sure you are."

She could feel his heat and smell the clean sweat of his body. The boys she'd dated at the university never seemed to sweat. The earthy smell seemed as exotic as everything else about the mining operation. She searched for something to say—something that would prove to him that she wasn't still twelve years old. Her eyes sought his. "So. Are you looking for another vein? Doing a little blasting maybe?"

"Did you stay up all night reading geological surveys?"

She pulled her hat down low and turned to survey the place. Darned if he would see her blush. "Everyone knows crystal veins run eight degrees north of true east-west. You just follow the vein to find the pockets," she said with as much authority as she could muster.

"Oh, well, then I'm sure everyone knows that the famous McEarl crystals do not run in veins at all, but in isolated pockets that are rather like looking for a needle in a haystack."

"I knew that." To her great relief he went back to his baskets before he could ask her some stupid question about how the crystals ever got into the ground to begin with. She'd only gotten through the introduction of Bulletin-whatever-it-was last night. She quickly walked over to the men squatting beside the cave.

"Hi. I'm Kristy. Virgil's granddaughter."

A young man scrambled out of the cave and grinned and muttered greetings. An older man stood up stiffly and smiled. "You wouldn't remember me, but I used to see you with your grandpa from time to time," the older man said. "I'm Arvin, this here's my grandson, Wesley."

Their clothes were stiff with the sticky clay, and Kristy found herself wondering how on earth they ever got them clean. "Hi. Found any good ones?"

"A few," Arvin said.

Arvin rubbed some of the clay off an egg-sized rock and handed it to her. "Double-terminator."

Kristy examined the crystal. It was dull with clay, but she could see the natural point at both ends. It amazed her that something this dull and ordinary looking would turn into a brilliant, gleaming crystal once it was cleaned. "Nice." She rubbed the crystal with the tail of her shirt. "Can I dig some?"

Arvin grinned, and Wesley handed her what looked like a crow bar that had been straightened out. "You bet. We'll show you just how she's done."

She meant to ask the men about Virgil and his disappearing acts, but instead spent the next half hour squatted in the cave, carefully digging in the clay under a constant stream of instruction from Arvin. She managed to cut her finger twice on sharp points, but she forgot all about the pain and squealed with delight when she pried out a nice cluster. As she scraped the clay away to see what she had, a sense of timelessness swept over her. The cluster she held had lain in its nest of clay for some 200 million years, unseen, untouched by the hand of man. Her hands trembled at the thought, and in that moment a bit of crystal fever stole into her blood.

Her thoughts were pulled back to her surroundings when all the machinery stopped and a strange quietness settled over the mine. The only sound came from Mercury, sitting at the edge of the pit, howling. When she turned around, the men were gathering in the shade created by the pit wall, lunch pails in hand. She didn't want to stop digging, but she knew the men would want to eat, so she carefully wrapped her crystal cluster in a piece of newspaper and stood up.

"That was absolutely fantastic. Can I come and dig with you again?"

Wesley shuffled from one foot to the other. Arvin grinned. "You bet you can. Any granddaughter of Virgil's is welcome as can be. We can teach you all there is to know about these rocks."

She waved and went to find Mike, who was standing straight and rigid beside the track loader, watching her. "My, my, the prodigal granddaughter does have her devoted followers. Just like her father before her."

The bitterness in his voice shocked her. "What does my father have to do with this?"

"I'm sure you can figure it out," he said and walked off.

She shrugged and followed him back to the track loader, where he began to hoist baskets of crystals into the gigantic bucket. One of the men abandoned his lunch to help. Kristy picked up a basket and struggled under its weight. Mike took it away from her and swung it up into the bucket as if it were full of feathers.

"I thought you wanted to be a foreman. Foremen don't load rocks," he whispered loudly. "They supervise."

"Your words, Mike, not mine." She glared at him, very much aware that he was trying to intimidate her with his mocking. His eyes were still that annoying shade of open-sea blue, and she thought she might very well drown in them right then and there. He turned away before she could decide. She wandered over to Arvin and Wesley.

"You guys have any idea when Granddad will be back?"

They shook their heads. "I sure thought he'd be back by now. Me and Wesley was wonderin' about him just this morning," Arvin said. Then he lowered his voice. "I think Virgil's out lookin' for them rocks him and Chester buried back durin' the war."

Kristy stared at the older man. "What rocks?"

"Well, there's some don't put any stock in the story, but I remember when they hit that crystal pocket. Lord have mercy, I never seen such rocks. But now you keep that under your hat, ma'am. There's men'd kill for them rocks."

"You mean this mine is—"

"Shoot, in my opinion we're just killin' time here, Miss Kristy. Just killin' time."

"But—" Maybe Mr. Eldridge wasn't as far off base as she'd thought—but before she could discover anything more, she heard Mike calling. She ran to the track loader and almost managed to scramble up the enormous machine by herself, except for one quick boost from Mike. As soon as she wrapped her arm around the roll bar, she found him jammed up against her. Another man was driving the machine.

On the way up the steep incline, the machine bucked and burped along, as if it wanted to stay at the bottom. She had no choice but to lean against Mike, and that, along with the angle of the machine, made her feel her whole world was turning upside down. His arm circled her waist to steady her, but she thought he was holding her a little more tightly than necessary. At the feel of his body against her—the hard muscles, the thin shirt— memories of the motorcycle ride came back, except she was no longer twelve and Mike was no longer an obnoxious wiry teenager. Well, obnoxious, maybe, but . . . she was greatly relieved when she touched solid ground again. They loaded the baskets of crystals into the back of Mike's truck, and he took a chain out of the toolbox of the loader.

"Arvin and Wesley are really nice. *They* said I could dig with them anytime." Mercury sailed into the truck, and she climbed in with him.

"They've never had such a beautiful supervisor." His voice held the same edge she'd heard the night before. "How could I possibly compete with you for a place in the cave?"

She ignored the jab. "And they are worried about Virgil, even if you aren't. Arvin thinks he's gone off to find the crystals he and Chester buried during the war."

She sensed a sudden tension in Mike's hands on the steering wheel. "Is that old story making the rounds again?"

"Well . . ."

"There's nothing to it. It's like the old lost gold mine stories."

She started to ask more, but they had stopped beside her car, still safely perched in the ditch. Mike pulled the car out with no trouble using his pickup.

Kristy took a deep breath. "As long as I'm here, I might as well continue to help out. What else can I do?"

"Nothing."

"Nothing? You're spending ten thousand dollars a month and you can't use free labor? Sounds like a heck of a way to run a railroad."

"This railroad has done just fine without your help, and it will do just fine long after you're gone." His voice was soft, but as hard as steel.

She threw her hat on the ground. "Well this railroad is about to make some changes. I have grandfather's power of attorney, and for now we are partners, whether you like it or not, Mike Ferguson. Now you can tell me how I can help or I can figure it out." He looked as if she had slapped him.

"What are you talking about?"

"Power of attorney. You didn't know about it? Well maybe you don't know as much about my grandfather as you think you do."

His face turned dark red with anger. "Fine. You want to work? You can get your pretty little fanny to work cleaning all these crystals. It'll give you a chance to see how the other half makes their living. You do know how the oxalic acid bath works?"

"Yes, I do."

"Good. I'll see you at the house." He jumped in the truck and fishtailed his way down the mountain. Merc, she noted irritably, had chosen to ride with Mike.

She drove to Virgil's, wondering what all the fuss had been about. The power of attorney had upset him. That, coupled with his attempts to get rid of her, seemed suspicious at best, although of what she wasn't sure. But she intended to find out. She made a mental note to ask Mr. Eldridge about the lost crystals.

Mike was unloading the baskets when she parked her car next to his truck. The backyard was a jumble of huge rusty tanks and tables built of rough wood and close-mesh wire tops. The tables, all laden with crystals in various stages of cleaning, seemed to lean to the north as if one day they might all simply fall down at the same time, in the same direction.

Mike's jaw was set in a hard line, and this time he didn't object when she struggled with the baskets of crystals. "You put them on the wire tables and hose them off. Let the remaining clay dry, then hose them again. You keep doing that until you've cleaned off as much clay as you can. Assuming you last that long. Then they go into the oxalic acid."

"Right. And don't worry, I'll last, and I'll do it right." She wanted him to go away now. She was starving and she needed to think.

"I've tried to get Virgil to put in gas-fired tanks, but he says there's nothing like a wood fire to clean crystal." He nodded toward a huge stack of wood and arched his eyebrows.

"I know how to start a wood fire."

"Well, you have to watch it. Too hot and it fractures the crystals. Not hot enough and it doesn't clean."

"I get the picture." She unwrapped a large crystal point, spit on it and rubbed it on her shirt. The point caught the fire of the sun, and she gasped. "Oh, look at this one." She rubbed it again and held it up to the sun.

"And don't fall in love with all of them." He started for the truck.

"Wait a minute. Just how much money have you put in the mine you're working with Granddad?" He put his hands on the truck cab, exasperation written all over him.

"I don't think that's any of your business."

"And I think it is. Since we're temporary partners."

"Wrong, Kristy. We will never be partners."

She scrutinized him for a long moment. If Mr. Eldridge and Arvin were right, any investment was high risk. So why would he put money into the mine? "Why are you doing this?" she asked softly.

"Doing what?" he said in little more than a whisper.

"Putting money into an abandoned mine that nobody thinks has good crystals. According to Mr. Eldridge that mine hasn't been worked in years." When he didn't respond, she decided to push him a bit further. "Maybe even a sham, or a decoy for something else."

"If Virgil thinks there are crystals in that mine, then there are crystals," he said in a faraway voice, then seemed to shake himself, the spell broken. "You shouldn't believe everything you hear, but you can damn well believe this— I don't invest in empty holes." He yanked open the truck door. "I doubt you'd understand. I doubt it very much."

"Try me."

He crossed the distance between them, tipped her hat back and looked at her for what seemed an eternity. "No, Kristy. You gave up your right to ask questions years ago. Just like your father did. Go back to school. You don't belong here." Before she could respond, he was heading toward his truck again. "I'll bring another load of rocks tomorrow. And don't forget to feed Merc."

Then he was gone and she was left with the memory of his stinging words. She went to the house and ate a sandwich, then got to work unwrapping crystals from the newspaper coverings and going over everything Mike had said. Which was not much. What had happened between Mike and her father to sustain such bitterness over the years? Mike couldn't have been more than a boy when her father left Mount Ida. But something had happened, and she needed to know what, since he was smearing her with the same brush.

He obviously didn't think she had enough sense to run a hamburger stand, let alone help out with a mine, but that surely couldn't have anything to do with her father. Her father was an incredibly astute businessman. Well, she would have to figure it out. In the meantime, she thought there should be a law against men of questionable astrological signs having such wonderful blue eyes.

She hosed off the new crystals and then hosed off a few more tablefuls that had been started but not finished. The only sounds were those of her work, the breeze in the pine trees and a few birds that came to scold.

Sometime in the middle of the afternoon Mercury howled, and she looked up to see a man in a green and khaki uniform walking around the house. By now she was soaking wet and clay stained.

He tipped his hat, barely, but it was enough for her to see that he was going bald. "Hi. I'm John Graves. Forestry Service."

She wiped a hand on her jeans and shook hands. "Hi. I'm Kristy, Virgil's granddaughter. I'm kind of in a mess right now."

The man carefully examined some of the crystals she'd just unwrapped. "That's okay. It's a messy business. I just stopped to see if Virgil was back yet."

"No, he's off busying around somewhere." She waved in the general direction of the woods. "Can I help you?"

"No—just stopped to visit with Virgil."

"Well, you know Granddad," she said brightly.

"Funny. He wasn't over on the mountain yesterday where I thought he'd be."

Kristy felt the cold touch her again. "You think something might have happened to him?"

"Probably not. I guess Virgil knows these old mountains about as well as anybody. Well, you have a nice vacation."

"Uh, Mr. Graves, where *does* Granddad go out there? Have any idea?" She slipped her notebook out, licked the end of her pencil just like Virgil would and stood poised to take down all the information.

"Little bit of everywhere. Fisher Spur, Beck Mountain. Sometimes he goes over around Mount Ida Mountain, but mostly he stays pretty close to home. Five-, ten-mile radius."

Kristy wrote down all the possible sites after he left, then viciously hosed the clay from a table of crystals. She had one vote for Virgil safe, one vote missing and one vote maybe. She didn't know what to think.

By dark, Kristy had unwrapped and washed crystals until she thought she would drop. Before quitting, she loaded the washed crystals into the wire racks ready to go into the tanks of acid. She had dropped everything twice to answer the phone and reassure Mr. Eldridge, telling him that Virgil was not back but that she was sure he was all right and she would let the lawyer know the minute he returned.

A hot bath helped with her fatigue, but she wondered if she would even be able to get out of bed in the morning.

She finally ate a can of soup and a peanut butter sandwich, fed Mercury and piled up in the bed with a topographical map of the area, her notepad and the Geological Survey. She carefully located all the places John Graves had mentioned and drew two circles in a five-mile and ten-mile radius. She wasn't sure what all the green splotches and squiggly lines on the map meant, but she was sure that looking for Virgil in that much territory would be like looking for a needle in a haystack. She would have to start with the named mountains. If she could find them.

While she was struggling to keep her eyes open, it occurred to her that Mike could probably go out and find her grandfather in a minute if he wanted to. Why he didn't want to, nagged at her. She again sensed that something wasn't quite right, but she couldn't put her finger on anything specific. She hated to admit it, but her suspicions of him trying to take Virgil's mine or steal from him were, at this point, very weak. Underneath the anger in his voice, she'd heard love when he talked about her grandfather. And a loyalty to Virgil so intense it was frightening.

Her last thought before falling asleep was that Mike had very cleverly managed to tie her to the house—or more specifically to the tables and cleaning tanks. He would no doubt appear at daylight with his stupid track loader *full* of crystals. And his wonderful hair all clean and brushed and his blue eyes mocking her and . . .

Sometime in the night, Kristy thought she heard a monstrous clap of thunder, but there was only the one, and the rain never came.

CHAPTER FIVE

KRISTY STRUGGLED out of bed well before sunrise, so stiff and sore she could hardly move, but she wasn't about to let Mike catch her lounging in the bed. She would have all the tanks going by the time he arrived with his load of rocks. Yesterday she would not have dreamed of calling the lovely crystals rocks, but after a day of handling hundreds of pounds of them, she caught herself using the local term. Maybe they were rocks until they were cleaned or something.

As a child she had loved the little crystals she carted home at the end of every summer. She pretended they were diamonds and lavished them on her best friends at school. She supposed it had never occurred to her that the crystals were her grandfather's livelihood. It had all been a wonderful game, a treasure hunt.

By the time the gray light of morning touched the backyard, she was busy. Fortunately all four tanks were filled with a greenish, murky liquid so she didn't have to worry about figuring out the proper mix. She donned the long, rubber gloves she found and lowered the wire racks full of crystals into the liquid. By the time the eastern sky turned a rosy pink, she had fires going under all the tanks. Little fires. She piled on more wood and watched the little fires suddenly change to big fires. Big, hot fires. The kind of fires that would fracture all those beautiful crystals she had worked so hard to clean.

Panicked by the thought of all her lovely crystals shattered into millions of pieces, she ran to the ramshackle shed behind the house and grabbed a rake. By the time she dragged a few burning logs out from under each tank, the leaves and pine needles around the first tank were burning merrily. She dropped the rake and snatched up a hose, which defied all her attempts to straighten out its tangles. Precious minutes passed before she got it unwound and hooked up to the tap, giving the bright fingers of fire time to reach in new directions, burning trails over the entire back yard. She yelled at the fire—why, she couldn't imagine—and sprayed and yelled and sprayed until nothing burned except four rather pitiful fires under the four tanks.

In spite of the cool, dewy morning, she was drenched with sweat and covered with ash and black soot. She very carefully placed one small log on each fire and sat down on a stump, rake in one hand, hose in the other. She never remembered this kind of problem with the fires at camp. But then, she had never gotten past building fires for roasting marshmallows. She made a mental note to call the gas company and get a quotation for Virgil on having gas burners put under the tanks.

She began to relax a little as the fires burned where they were supposed to, but inside she was still a wreck. She wanted a cup of coffee in the worst way, but she was afraid if she went to the house, the whole county would be on fire when she came out.

Just as the morning sun touched the tops of the pine trees, she heard Mike's truck. She wanted to jump up and at least wash off the soot and dirt that covered her, but she couldn't seem to get off her stump, and besides, it was too late. She turned in time to see the pickup back up to the wire tables.

Mike stepped out of the truck and calmly surveyed the scene. She refused to look at him, and she couldn't tell whether his silence came from anger or an attempt to keep from bursting into raucous laughter. If she heard so much as one snigger, she was going to bludgeon him with the rake and possibly finish him off by strangling him with the hose.

"Well, it looks like you've got everything under control this morning, Kristy," he said in a neutral tone as he began to shift baskets of crystals. "You *do* seem to have a knack with wood fires."

"Don't say it. Just don't, I repeat, *do not* say one word to me."

He finished unloading the truck and gingerly touched the side of each tank, then poked the fires with a stick and added more wood. "It's all in the seasoning of the wood. This wood is a little dry so it burns hot and fast."

"Really? I hadn't noticed," she said, clutching her rake and hose. She knew her face must be black with soot. She rubbed it against the sleeve of her T-shirt as best she could without letting go of her fire-fighting tools.

"What we need is a little green wood to slow it down." He went to a pile of wood that looked the same as the other piles of wood, carefully selected a few logs and put them on the fires, then glanced at the tables, a puzzled look on his face. "You cleaned all those rocks last night?"

"Every one of them."

"Are you sure you got the clay off?" He took a long stick and removed the lid from one of the tanks and peered into the simmering liquid.

"Yes, I am sure I got all the clay off. I did not put filthy rocks into the tanks."

"Hmmm. I didn't think you'd get that far," he muttered, more to himself than to her.

"Well, I did. And I did it just like I was supposed to. Until I got to the fire part."

She was trying very hard to ignore him, but suddenly he was standing over her. He licked his thumb and rubbed her cheek. "Your face is dirty. Again."

She thought it was time to bludgeon him, but she couldn't seem to move. All she could do was think about his thumb rubbing the smudges off her face. "I am perfectly capable of washing my own face," she sputtered.

"Ummm, so I see. I don't suppose you made any coffee?" He started for the house.

She jumped up from the stump and waved the rake at his retreating back. "No, I did not make any coffee. I was too busy setting the woods on fire."

"You'll find some folding chairs in the shed," he called over his shoulder. "I'll be right back." He evidently sensed she wasn't moving. "You can let go of the rake and hose."

She threw down her tools and went to rummage in the shed for chairs. The ones she found didn't look very safe, but she dragged them out into the yard anyway, then hurriedly splashed her face with water and scrubbed it as best she could. The cold water felt good, but the cooler she got, the more annoyed she became—with herself for not being able to handle a few stupid fires, with Mike for catching her in such a mess. And she despised herself for feeling such relief that he was there in case anything else happened. When he came out the back door carrying two mugs of coffee, she was perched in her chair as if she had spent her life watching fires and tanks of crystals.

She took a sip of scalding coffee. It was strong, the way she liked it. ''So how long do I keep the fires going?''

''Depends on how dirty the crystals are. These weren't too bad, so I'd say maybe feed the fires two more times, then just let them burn out. You can check the crystals when the acid cools off, see what they look like. Sometimes you have to cook a few of them a second time.''

''Okay.'' She waited for him to say something else, but he drank his coffee in silence, and Kristy couldn't think of a thing to say to him. Oh, she could think of a million things to ask him, another million or so things they should talk about, but the strange quietness of the pine forest settled around her, and she leaned back and let the sounds of the insects and early-morning birds wash over her. A bluejay came to scold them from a branch overhead. Mike slouched down in one of the rickety chairs and stared at the fire. He almost looked relaxed. Kristy stared at the fire, mesmerized by the flames and her exhaustion.

''Virgil had three more tanks here at one time. Big tanks. Thousand gallon ones.''

She jumped at the sound of his voice. ''I thought there used to be more.'' She vaguely remembered more of something in the backyard.

''He burned them up.''

Kristy smiled and scooted farther down in her chair. ''You're kidding.''

''Nope. Damn near burned up the house and the woods with them.'' Kristy sipped her coffee and waited for him to continue.

"He had a bunch of big plates."

"Plates?"

"Big clusters of crystal. Heavy, with some of the rock attached to the bottom. Anyway, these were big ones. Three and four feet across, bristling with foot-long points so clear you could read a newspaper through them. It took a block and tackle to move them from the truck into the tanks. Late fall, dry as tinder. Granddad and I were helping him. Chester kept saying, 'Virgil, you can't clean these things in weather like this, you'll burn ever'thing from here to Texas.' Virgil kept saying, 'Dammit, Chester, I been cookin' rocks thirty years and I, by God, oughta' know when you can cook 'em.'" Mike chuckled. "To hear those two talk, you'd have thought they were sworn enemies. Well, just about the time they got the fires hot, the wind shifted. A blistering wind right out of the south." He pointed to two enormous pine trees at the edge of the woods. "See those black scars? We fought that fire with wet tow sacks until it got to the woods. I was never so scared in my life."

She looked at the trees and could almost see the two old men and one frightened boy desperately trying to stop a fire. "So what happened?"

"Granddad finally called the forestry service. They put it out and lectured Virgil severely about fires and prevailing weather conditions. Virgil managed to blame the blaze on them for not notifying everyone of a possible wind shift."

Kristy laughed. "And he probably got away with it, didn't he?"

"Yeah, he did."

Kristy again heard that mixture of love and fierce loyalty in his voice. It was only there when he talked about Virgil, and it made her feel warm and nice all over. She knew that somewhere deep inside him was a man the likes of which she had never known, and she wanted to know more about the relationship between him and her grandfather. She knew it went far beyond any business partnership, but sensed it went even deeper than friendship. She felt a twinge of jealousy mingled with guilt that Mike was so close to her grandfather. It was a kind of closeness she had never experienced. She rested her head on the back of the chair. The smell of woodsmoke and pine, pleasant conversation...she could see herself spending a lifetime in this place, prying the treasured bits of rock from the earth and transforming them into things of beauty for the world to enjoy. She imagined she and her grandfather...and Mike working together, living side by side. That thought snapped her to attention.

"So. What are you doing in school?"

Kristy shrugged and stared at the fires. "School? Oh. Art history this semester."

"Art history? What do you do with art history?"

"Good question. But, then, I never figured out what you did with food science of philosophy or journalism or algology."

"Algology?"

"The study of algae. Strange, fascinating little creatures, but not what I wanted to devote my life to."

"And just what do you want to devote your life to?"

She sighed and returned her attention to the fires. The fires and Mike's voice had a hypnotic effect. "I wish I knew. I figure I'll know it when I find it."

"Like a bolt of lightning striking?"

"Mmm, I keep hoping. Astrology's close, but the career opportunities seem a bit limited." She stretched her legs and hoped the chair wouldn't collapse. He was actually being pleasant, treating her like a grown-up, and they weren't fighting.

"I somehow don't think rocks will be your calling. They must be boring for someone with such a varied background."

"Nothing's boring. At least not until you know enough about it. Everything's interesting for a while." She closed her eyes.

"Including crystals and charging around on your white horse to rescue people who don't need rescuing?"

The change in his tone penetrated her groggy mind. His pleasant, rich voice had assumed that hard edge again. "That's not what I meant. I was talking about—" The phone rang before she could finish her explanation. She ran into the house and snatched it up. "Hello?"

"Miss Kristy? This is Samuel Eldridge."

"Oh. Hi, Mr. Eldridge."

"I hate to be a pest this early in the morning, but there was trouble in the night, and I thought you should know about it."

"Trouble? What kind of trouble?"

"The important thing is that no one was hurt."

Kristy wanted to hurry the lawyer, but she had learned he didn't hurry well at all. "What happened?"

"Well, someone did a bit of midnight dynamiting over west of Virgil's mine last night."

"Dynamite? You mean like, blew up something?"

The lawyer paused. "Well, yes, my dear, that is generally what dynamite is used for. Of course, they were long gone by this morning. The forest rangers can't tell that anything was taken. But there was a rather large hole and signs of digging. Not that this has anything to do with Virgil, Miss Kristy, I wouldn't alarm you for the world, but I don't like it. I don't like it one bit.''

Dynamite? Kristy couldn't believe people were running around with dynamite, let alone using it. "Of course not, and I'm sure Granddad is just fine." Bless his heart, Mr. Eldridge sounded well past alarmed. ''And thanks for calling. I guess you can let me know if there's anything I can do." What could one do about a dynamited hillside? "Oh, Mr. Eldridge, I wanted to ask you something. Did Granddad ever talk about some crystals—you know, great big ones—that he and Chester found during the war?''

"Oh, dear, who told you?"

"I heard something about it at the mine."

"That's what I've been afraid of."

She could almost hear him fidgeting and fussing. "Then they do exist?"

"Of course they exist, except it's supposed to be a secret, but I'm afraid everyone in the world knows about them. They would be worth a fortune in today's market. I just hope Virgil has not told too many people." A long pause followed. "Well, let me hear from you, my dear."

Kristy stood staring at nothing while she tried to sort things out. Mr. Eldridge and Arvin both believed there were lost crystals, but Mike denied it. So who was right? And if the crystals did exist, why did Mike want her to think they were just the subject of lost gold mine tales? And what did any of it have to do with Virgil being off in the woods? And the dynamiting...the dynamiting! She hurried outside to break the news to Mike. While she was horrified at the thought of anyone dynamiting a hillside, the fact that she finally knew something Mike didn't pleased her. She relayed her information and noticed that Mike didn't even bother to shift in his chair, let alone get upset. "Well?" she demanded.

"I've already been out and checked the situation. Nothing was taken. They didn't even haul off any of the rocks."

She stared at him, hands on her hips. "You knew about it? And you didn't bother to tell me?"

He looked up. "It's just poachers. Goes with the territory these days."

Kristy felt her blood pressure rise. "You mean Mr. Eldridge called you first?" She didn't believe that for a minute.

"Sam probably found out over coffee at the café this morning. A ranger called me."

She took a deep breath. "We're partners. At least for the time being. I should know about these things."

Mike stood up, tossed the dregs of his coffee on the ground and gave her a hard look. "And what would you do about it? Go out and patrol the mountains at night? Go shovel all the dirt back into the hillside?"

She waved an accusing hand at him. "Well, I might do something, which is more than you seem to be doing."

"I don't play cops and robbers, Kristy, and you better not play that game either. This isn't something to add to your collection of experiences," he said sharply. "If something needs to be done, I'll take care of it—like I did before you came. Like I'll do when you're gone."

"Civilized people don't run around dynamiting things. The culprits need to be locked up."

"Oh, you have a lot to learn about this business, Kristy. A lot. But I'm sure you'll get bored long before you learn even the basics." With that, he turned and began throwing baskets of crystals out of his truck. "I'll have another load tonight or first thing in the morning."

"And while we're on the subject, since you won't tell me, you might tell Mr. Eldridge where Granddad is so he will quit worrying and quit driving me crazy every fifteen minutes."

He set a basket down very slowly, then straightened up and looked at her, his eyes narrowed to slits. "How many times do I have to tell you, I don't know. Sam worries about everything and everybody. He loves to worry." He tossed the last basket out of the truck. "These woods are crawling with rangers and hikers and loggers, Kristy. If anything has happened, someone would have found Virgil. No one has, so that means he is fine and does not want to be found."

Before she could respond, the truck was gone.

She checked the fires, stomped around in the burned area and in general wanted to throw something at someone, preferably a rock at Mike Ferguson. It wasn't any of her business...nothing she could do about it. She shouldn't worry her pretty head about things like dynamite. Well, people who could ignore other people dynamiting hillsides in the middle of the night were as crazy as the people with the dynamite. And she knew, just as well as she knew her own name, that Mike knew where Virgil was and for some reason wasn't telling her. And it had something to do with what? Her father? The story of the lost crystals? She sat down on the stump and tried to think it through. Mike acted as if he were jealous at times. Jealous of her? Surely not. Yet . . . she thought back over the angry remarks and accusations he had hurled at her. Was he afraid she would in some way take his place in Virgil's affections? She wished she

knew more about what had happened between her father and Virgil, and how Mike got involved in the rift.
She thought the answer lay somewhere in those years
they had all left behind.

When Mercury wandered through the yard in search
of a cool place, she jumped up from the stump and
latched onto him. "Just the one I've been looking for,
Merc old boy. It's bath time. Get rid of the stink time,
son." She tied him to a tree so he couldn't escape while
she went to get some soap. There was no liquid soap and
certainly nothing resembling dog shampoo, so in the
end she decided a little Giorgio bath gel might be just
the thing.

When she came out with the soap and a towel, Mercury looked as if he might just fade away from being so
pitiful. "Good grief, Merc, I'm not going to torture
you. It's just a lousy bath. It won't take a minute." He
showed no signs of believing her. "We're going to
Fisher Spur tonight to look for Granddad. Won't that
be nice? A nice ride in the car, maybe find nice Granddad?" She couldn't believe she was trying to coax him
into the bath as she might a child.

After giving great study to the size of the dog and the
size of the washtub hanging on the back porch, Kristy
decided the hose was the only way to go. The sun was
warm, so he shouldn't get a chill, not that Mercury
would even know what a chill was. After all, he wasn't
some delicate little house dog.

When the water from the hose touched him, the dog
collapsed in a great heap on the ground and refused to
move. She wet and scrubbed one side, then rolled him
over and wet and scrubbed the other side. Of course by
then the first side was filthy again, so she rolled him and
hosed off the first side again. It was rather like trying to

bathe a sack of cement. Somewhere in the middle of it all, he sprang to his feet and shook, then collapsed again.

"Nice, Merc, really nice shot. If you'd stand up, it would be a lot easier on both of us." The dog whined and refused even a tiny wag of his tail. By now Kristy was certain she had more water and shampoo on herself than on the dog, but she was determined. She pulled up his front end, but when she hefted his rear end from the ground, the front end collapsed again. After she tried that a few times, she didn't think she even cared whether he was clean or not.

"I give up, Merc," she finally said and unbuckled his collar. She would have to dry it and oil it before she put it back on him. Or buy him a new one. The minute the collar was off, the dog stood up, shook water all over her again and took off. Within minutes he had thrown himself in the ashes left from the fire, a pile of dirt near the edge of the woods and the remnants of Virgil's garden. When, a few minutes later, he loped off into the woods, Kristy couldn't even tell what color he was.

"That's not nice, Mercury. And if you roll in something really disgusting, you're banned from the house and car forever," she yelled at him. "And you won't get to go look for Granddad tonight."

Since he hadn't given her a chance to towel him off, she used the towel on herself and the sopping collar. When she unsnapped the dog tags, she noticed a small cylinder hanging on the ring with the rabies tag. It looked like one of those little cylinders they attached to homing pigeons' legs. She twisted the ends and the holder came apart . . . to reveal a tightly rolled piece of paper.

She carefully unrolled the damp paper and smoothed it out. The lettering was faded, as if written by an old pencil stub.

Sure as hell hope this hound makes it this time. Out of food, out of water, out of everything. Indians everywhere!

The writing was her grandfather's. She shivered in spite of the hot sun.

She took the note to the porch and sat down, desperately trying to figure out when it had been written and what it meant. It had to be a joke or a code, and she was in no mood for jokes right now.

Kristy's first impulse was to call the sheriff; her second was to find Mike. She did neither, knowing there would be lengthy explanations, and in the end both men would no doubt assure her that everything was just hunky-dory and that Virgil would be back any minute. Well, she was tired being patted on the head and told to go play with her crystals. And she was tired of Mike's empty assurances. She wanted her grandfather. Alive and breathing and close enough to touch.

And if he wasn't alive and breathing, she wanted to know that, too. She carefully refolded the paper and walked into the woods in search of Mercury. If anyone could find Virgil, it was his beloved hound.

She found the dog half-submerged in a stagnant pond a half mile or so from the house. He refused her entreaties for him to come out. "I'm sorry, Merc, I'll never wash you again. Please, this is important." He smiled his doggy smile and finally lumbered toward her. She didn't even scold him when he rubbed most of the stagnant goop on her jeans.

She bent down and held his face in her hands. "I want you to find Granddad, Merc. Virgil. Where's Virgil?" She stood up and pointed to the woods. "Go find him, boy." The dog sat and smiled and wriggled his body. Kristy felt the beginnings of panic nibble at her mind.

She walked away from the dog, into the woods by herself. Mercury followed beside her. "Please, Merc, help me." She cupped her hands to her mouth. "Granddad," she yelled. A hollow echo came back to her, and the silence of the forest settled on them again.

Before an hour passed, she had yelled until she was hoarse, Mercury had abandoned her for several rabbits, and her panic had turned to tears, then to anger. She had pushed away the thoughts that Virgil was dead somewhere out there. She told herself he was hurt, unable to get back, waiting for someone to come. But after an hour in the woods, Kristy knew she would never find Virgil, not if she tramped around these mountains for the rest of her life. There was just too much ground to cover. An organized search was what it would take, and that's exactly what she was going to demand.

She left Mercury to his rabbits and started back to the house. She would take the note to Mike, and he would darn well do something this time. Not even Mike Ferguson could explain this away.

CHAPTER SIX

KRISTY DROVE the BMW as hard as she dared on the twisting roads. When she screeched to a halt in a cloud of dust, Mike was standing beside the track loader, talking to Arvin and Wesley. He looked up and frowned, then came toward her.

"What happened? Did you burn the house down?"

She vaguely remembered she was covered with water and mud but didn't care. She would present her evidence calmly, but she would not brook any more pats on the head. She wanted action. "We need a search party," she started. "It will be a lot easier if you organize it because you know everyone, but if you won't, I will."

Mike's frown deepened. "What are you talking about?"

"I found a note." She felt the tears well up.

He put one hand on her shoulder, the other under her chin and made her look at him. "Just calm down and tell me what you're talking about."

His voice was calm, but she saw fear flicker in his eyes then disappear as quickly as it had come. It was enough to make the tears come. She fell into his arms and clung to him, letting his strong hands soothe her. "Oh, Mike, I'm afraid we're too late."

He gently pushed her away and wiped a tear from her cheek. "Kristy, let me see the note."

She fumbled in her pocket for the crumpled paper and handed it to him. "It's some kind of code. I figured you'd know what it meant."

Mike carefully smoothed out the note and read it. As he did, she noticed that he began to relax. "Kristy, this is nothing. It's a game we play with Mercury." He waved the paper at her and smiled. "We were trying to teach Merc to carry notes. It seemed like a good idea in case something happened to Virgil out in the woods. Virgil would write something, any crazy thing, and put it in the tube. I'd check it and give Merc a dogbone. It didn't work very well. Merc forgot where he was going, or—"

She wiped her face. "Do you really expect me to believe a cock and bull story like that?"

His eyes hardened. "Yes, I do. It's the truth."

"You didn't check his collar last night."

"We gave up on Merc weeks ago."

She walked in a circle, thinking. "The theory behind the game is that the dog always goes with Virgil, right? If something happens, Granddad puts the note in the collar, and Merc brings it back to you or someone at the house, right?"

"Right."

She looked him in the eye, her voice soft but with its own edge. "So why isn't Mercury with Virgil on this trip?"

There was a long moment of silence. "Because Virgil was going most of the way on foot. He didn't want to carry dogfood in a backpack."

Kristy was the first to break eye contact. It all sounded so logical when he said it, so right. Yet, she knew he was holding back some part, maybe all, of the truth. "Mike, where is he? Why won't you tell me?"

"I don't know where he is, Kristy. All I know is that he is fine."

"How could you possibly know that?"

He shrugged. "Because I have no evidence to the contrary. Now go home and clean your crystals and quit worrying. Virgil will be back any day now."

There seemed nothing else to do or say, and suddenly that fact annoyed her more than anything. "Either you care more about this stupid mine than you do about Granddad or you're trying to keep me from seeing him. Either way, I'm sick and tired of being patronized. If you can't give me one good reason why I shouldn't within the next five seconds, then I'm going to call in the biggest darn search party this county has ever seen, and I'm going to find Granddad. Whether he wants to be found or not."

The muscles in his jaw twitched. "Leave Virgil alone."

"I'm going to take this note to the sheriff for openers."

"No, Kristy. You're going to mind your own business. If you go to the sheriff, I'll be right behind you, and I'll tell him you're a hysterical college girl from the city, meddling in Virgil's business. And that will be the end of it."

She looked at the faraway mountains, buying time as that nagging feeling about secrets and jealousy touched her again. Perhaps it was time to get everything into the open. "What are you afraid of, Mike? Granddad has enough love for both of us."

His face turned as dark as a spring thunderhead. "I'm not worried about whether he has enough love, but whether he has too much. You don't see Virgil for *years*. If you're so damned concerned about him, why haven't you been to see him? You roar in here out of nowhere and start meddling in his business and mine. And you'll no doubt roar off one day the same way. What the hell do you expect? Do you expect people to put their lives on hold while you decide what you want to be when you grow up?''

He was throwing her own words back at her. "No, but I expect to be treated like a woman who is very much afraid for her grandfather."

He pointed a finger at her. "Do you think for one minute that I wouldn't be tearing these mountains apart if I thought something had happened to him? I have known Virgil all my life." He stabbed the air with a rigid finger. "I'm the one who's worked with him. I'm the one who sat with him when he was sick. Not his family, Kristy. I did. Where the hell were *you* all those years? Where the hell was his son?" He took a deep breath and let it out slowly. "Now drop it, and leave us alone."

His harsh words cut her to the quick, but there was little question in her mind that he meant exactly what he said. Or that he had nursed bitter feelings toward Virgil's family for many years. Or that he would fight a buzz saw for Virgil. Mike Ferguson flat didn't want her to see Virgil, and his opposition went far beyond simple jealousy. He was afraid she would hurt Virgil, the same way he thought her father had.

Seeing the blazing anger in those blue eyes, she knew it was time to make Mike understand she loved Virgil and was only here to help him. "I don't know what happened between Daddy and Granddad, but it was none of my doing, and I won't take the blame. I was wrong to not come sooner, but if I can deal with that and Granddad can deal with it, that ought to be good enough for you. Two days, Mike. If he's not back in two days, I'll call in the troops. And if you think I can't manage that, just try me.'' They glared at each other for another long moment, then she saw him visibly relax, felt the tension drift off on the afternoon breeze. It was as if they had both let off steam and things would be fine until the pressure built again. Which, she had no doubt, it would.

"We'll see." He leaned close and sniffed. "I've never had a foreman who smelled so good. And so bad. All at the same time."

She tossed her head and turned to walk to her car. "It's Giorgio bath gel and stagnant pond yuck. Merc and I bathed each other."

The ghost of a smile played at his lips. "Good God, you bathed Merc in Giorgio?"

She returned his hint of a smile. "Well it's about time somebody added a little class to this operation."

"I can't wait to smell what dead rabbit does to the scent. It should be quite unique."

"Two days, Mike." She got in her car, slammed the door and careened down the mountain.

She spent the trip home deciding what to do about the note, about Mike, about things in general . . . especially about Mike. There was no question in her mind that Mike had been scared when she first told him about the note. She was sure she had seen concern in his eyes. But then he'd relaxed and totally discounted her fears. Which meant . . . what? He certainly wasn't trying to protect *her*. If there really *were* bad guys, Mike would probably deliver her to them with a red bow in her hair. Just to get rid of her. Which brought her back to the original problem of why. He was protecting Virgil— from her. Who did Mike Ferguson think he was, anyway?

By the time she got home, she had decided on a strategy. First, she had to convince Mike that she wasn't going to do anything to break Virgil's heart, that whatever had happened all those years ago had nothing to do with her. Second, she had to start being nice to Mike. Even if it killed her. She just hoped he wouldn't start being nice back. It would make him more attractive than she could bear. Third, she needed to enlist a little help in flushing Virgil out of hiding. Put a little outside pressure on Mike. She would call Mr. Eldridge and John Graves and ever so casually mention the note and let them go from there.

She dialed the lawyer's number. "Mr. Eldridge? This is Kristy." She told him about the note. "Do you think it means anything?"

There was a long silence. "Oh, dear. What does Michael say?"

"Michael assures me it's an old note, part of some game he and Virgil and the dog play."

"Well, now, I'll just have a word with Michael about that, and perhaps talk to the sheriff. I don't like this, Miss Kristy, I don't like this one bit, and you can rest assured that I will look into the situation."

She then placed a call to John Graves, who was out in the field and would get back to her.

Not sure what else she should do about Virgil—or Mike—she put together a cheese and tomato sandwich and went to the yard to eat it and check on the fires. They were burning down, and she hoped by dark she could look at the crystals in the tanks. It was like waiting for Christmas morning.

She wandered into the house and picked up the ring of keys on the desk. She might as well start on the rock shop. She gathered up the few cleaning supplies she could find and walked to the wire building. She got the padlock open on the third try and walked inside.

The building was made of poles, with a wavy tin roof and chicken wire for walls. It didn't look the least bit secure, but she supposed her grandfather didn't keep the really good stuff out here. The floor was a jumble of dusty cardboard boxes full of newspaper-wrapped crystals needing cleaning. Wire tables bristled with all sizes and shapes of rocks and crystals. Most looked as though they had been there for years—she supposed the only time the shop was open was when Virgil wasn't out looking for more crystals. Which made her wonder how he marketed the ones he found. She realized again just how little she knew about her grandfather and his business.

She had managed to wash most of the crystals on one table when a car pulled up. An older woman advanced on the open door like a ship under full sail, a younger woman following in her wake.

"Where is that dear man?" the older woman demanded.

"Mr. Cunningham is away for a few days," Kristy answered, a big smile on her face. Her first customers. "But I'm his granddaughter. Can I help you?"

"Oh, my dear, how lovely to meet you. We've been buying crystals from Virgil for eons. We've been by here a hundred times in the past week and were afraid we'd have to go back to Santa Fe without seeing him." She examined several of the clusters Kristy had just washed. "Lovely." She turned to the younger woman. "This one is warm. Feel it, Mary Alice?"

The younger woman closed her eyes and passed her hand over the crystal. "Nothing, Mother."

"Oh, dear." The woman walked among the tables, alternately closing her eyes and passing her hands over the tables. "We have a New Age shop outside Santa Fe. We don't take a thing to our customers that hasn't spoken to us."

Kristy smiled and swallowed any sales pitch she might have been thinking about. After all, she couldn't very well point out the ones that had spoken to her, since she hadn't heard a thing. While she watched the mother and daughter float through the building, listening and seeking signs of warmth, it occurred to her that she had no idea what to charge if they wanted any crystals. Panic began to nag at her. If she sold them too cheaply, Mike would have something else to yell about. Too high a price and she would lose her first customer. "Would you ladies excuse me a moment? Just feel free to look around. I'll be right back."

"Of course, my dear," the older woman said, an ethereal look on her face.

Kristy remembered halfway to the house that there was no phone at the mine. Not that she wanted to admit to Mike that she didn't have any idea of what to charge. The phone rang before she could decide who else to call. It was John Graves.

She quickly told him about the note.

"Mike's probably right. Virgil's been trying to train that dog since he was a pup." Kristy sighed. She was getting tired of Mike always being right. "But I agree, Virgil ought to be back by now. I'll pass the word to the paper companies and the rest of the men to keep a quiet eye out for him, Miss Cunningham. If he's not back in another day or two, we'll call in the state and local boys."

"Thanks so much. I'm really worried."

"I'll be in touch."

"Oh, before I let you go, I have a little problem. I don't guess you'd know how much to charge for crystals, do you? I have a customer and, well, I'm not sure what to do about it."

He chuckled. "That's real hard to say. Depends on a lot of things. Quality, clearness, the point— I'm not sure what to tell you. I think you need to talk to Mike."

"I can't get hold of Mike, and these ladies are hot to buy. Just as soon as something talks to them."

He laughed loudly. "I know the type. I wish I could help you, Miss Cunningham, but I don't know that much about Virgil's rocks. I guess twenty dollars a pound would be safe for anything Virgil's got."

"Thanks, that sounds good to me." She hung up the phone and quickly looked out the front window. The two women were still listening for messages and floating about.

She hurried back to the rock shop, feeling not really confident but at least a little better.

"Oh, there you are, my dear. Where are the good ones? In the cookers?"

"Well, they're not really ready to take out. I just started them this morning." She couldn't believe what she was saying. It seemed like months since she had almost burned down the woods. Kristy realized how exhausted she was.

"Nonsense. Let's have a look."

Before Kristy could say a word, the woman was steaming toward the tanks. Then she was running water into the tanks to cool the acid bath. Then she was lifting out a tray of crystals. They caught the fire of the late-afternoon sun and glittered like diamonds.

The woman shook a finger at Kristy. "You're a naughty girl, hiding these. I'll take this rack. Now let's have a look at the others."

Kristy took the racks out of the tanks and hosed them off. The woman seemed to be in fits of ecstasy and said they were *all* speaking to her. "By the way, dear, the last time I spoke to your dear grandfather, he told me he expected to have a new mine by this summer." She leaned over the rack she had just set down and whispered loudly. "'Big crystals,'" he said. "'Top quality.'"

Kristy smiled. She could hear Virgil whispering such a tidbit to this woman.

"Well, my dear, I have a very good friend, a superbly talented guru, who has received word that she must build a temple of crystals." She made motions with her hands. "Not a huge temple, you understand, just a tiny one."

Kristy listened in fascination. "The whole thing out of crystals? Who told her?"

"Her crystal, of course. Silly girl."

"Oh."

"The crystals must be the finest. She might like to buy all of Virgil's production. If it's good. I could look at the mine and—"

"Uh, you'd have to talk to Granddad."

"Well, I hope he hurries back. This woman is desperate for good crystals."

Desperate enough to steal them? flashed, unbidden, through Kristy's mind. The lost crystals came to mind.

"Even as we speak, she has people in this area looking. But of course if I found the right ones—"

You'd make the money on them, Kristy started to say then thought better of it. "We'll see."

Meanwhile the daughter had brought newspapers and boxes and begun to wrap the clusters. Kristy had had about all she could enjoy from this pair. This woman was obviously an Aries, heavy into Mars, her ruling planet. "Now wait just a minute. I haven't weighed them."

The mother gave her a shrewd look. "Going by the pound, are you? Virgil always priced them by the piece. He could tell at a glance. These aren't worth a penny over eight dollars a pound."

Kristy noticed that the ethereal New Age mystic had suddenly turned into a calculating businesswoman. And of course, just at that moment, Mike drove his truck in with another load. "Madam, there are thirty-dollar-a-pound rocks in there, and none are worth less than fifteen. Excuse me."

She hurried over to Mike. "What am I supposed to charge? There aren't prices on any of them."

"I thought you knew all about the business," he growled.

"Not a penny over twelve," the woman called.

"Not a penny under twenty," Kristy called back.

"You seem to be doing just fine," Mike whispered and continued unloading rocks.

"Fifteen."

"Seventeen," Kristy snapped. "Is that too much or too little," she whispered to Mike.

"Too little if she buys a few, okay if she takes them all."

"Done," the woman yelled, "and if Virgil is not here next time, I don't intend to buy a thing. You, young woman, are a robber."

Kristy smiled and went to get a set of scales she had noticed in the house. The three racks of crystals weighed out at seventy-three pounds and the woman counted out twelve hundred and forty-one dollars, mostly in new one-hundred-dollar bills. Kristy stared at the bills in awe, then jammed them in her pocket and helped wrap the goods.

The woman gave Mike a good once-over look. "Young man, I don't suppose *you* have a mine you'd like to sell."

"No, ma'am. I just work for this lady."

Kristy almost broke out laughing at his drawling, country accent. When the women and their crystals were gone, she shook her head. "That woman would kill for a few good rocks." When he didn't answer, she waved the money at him. "What do I do with this?"

Mike shook his head. "You might try banking it."

"I don't believe it. All this money for rocks? No wonder poaching is rampant."

"That woman will go home and sell those *rocks* for three to five times what she paid."

"You're kidding."

"Nope. And every one of them will have spoken personally to her. By the time she puts them in her shop, she will probably have dug them all herself, directed by some sort of divine guidance."

"Are the buyers all like that?"

"No, but we get our fair share. With any new movement like New Age, you get a lot of real believers, you get a goodly share of crazies, and then you get promoters and the con artists. You just got a good dose of the last."

Kristy was more than a little repulsed by the whole idea of selling the crystals to the woman. She wanted *her* crystals to go to people who would enjoy them for their beauty. "And where do you fit into all of this?"

"I'm the supplier. I don't require credentials from buyers."

Kristy thought for a moment. "But the New Age thing is relatively recent. What would those crystals have brought ten years ago?"

Mike shrugged. "A few dollars in shops. Maybe fifty cents a pound for industrial use."

"So why did people keep digging them?"

He shrugged. "It's a living."

Kristy knew that was no kind of answer. "Right. Uh, you want to go through the shop and give me some pointers on pricing?"

"I don't have time right now. Whatever you can get is fine."

Kristy started to snap at him then bit her tongue. She was going to be nice. "Granddad worked hard to dig these crystals. I'm not going to *give* them away. I want him to have what they're worth. If I can't do that, I won't sell any."

He gave her a strange look. "My, my, we are taking our responsibility seriously, aren't we?"

"Yes, we are, because it is serious."

"Why? It's no skin off your nose if you don't get Virgil a fair price."

"Because it's—look, do you want to talk pricing or do you want me at the mine in the morning?"

"Heaven help me. We'll talk pricing."

She followed him to the rock shop, forcing her irritation to a controllable level.

He walked among the tables and showed her the finer points of quality and color and shape and how each affected price. She listened and absorbed the information, but a question nibbled at the edge of her mind like a squirrel worrying a nut. She wanted him to give her an answer, because somewhere in that answer lay an understanding of this man and of her grandfather. "Why, Mike? Why do you dig crystals?"

He took her hand and placed her fingers on each of the six sides of a large point. "Because it's what crystal diggers do, Kristy," he said softly. "Feel the tiny ridges? Crystals from Fisher Mountain have a little bit different ridges than the ones from Miller Mountain, or from Virgil's mine. The smoother they are, the better the quality."

She closed her eyes and felt the ridges, felt his hand guiding hers over the point, sensed his body near hers.

"McEarl crystals and ones from the old Coleman mine generally don't have ridges. They're as smooth as glass."

She pulled her hand from his and picked up a small cluster with a four inch crystal point leaning against a two inch one. She rubbed it on her shirt until it shone. "So this one is worth more because it's clearer, and because it's not chipped and because it's smoother and..."

He reached around her to take the crystal. She was again all too aware of him, his smell, his lean body, his single-minded devotion to these strange bits of rock, which had been formed when these mountains were heaved into place by a cataclysmic shift of the earth 200 million or more years ago.

"Only the last inch or so of this one is clear, so that's a minus. But if you look closely—" He held the crystal up to her eyes so the last rays of the evening sun would catch it. "There's a large fracture near the point. That's also a minus, except this particular fracture creates a rainbow."

As he slowly turned the crystal in front of her, a perfect rainbow twinkled at Kristy from deep inside the crystal. She forgot all about business and squealed with delight. When she moved the crystal, the rainbow moved and disappeared and winked back.

"Rainbows are a plus," he whispered.

His breath touched her ear, and she shivered with another kind of delight and realized she was leaning against him. She held the crystal toward the sun for one last look at the rainbow. "There are rainbows on the floor of the house every afternoon. But this one's inside." The rainbow shimmered and died as the sun dropped behind the tall scarred pine tree. "So how much is this one worth?" she asked in a dreamy voice.

"Five wholesale, ten by itself." He turned her around and smoothed her hair away from her face. "Ten dollars isn't much to see a rainbow every day, is it?"

"You love them, don't you?" she said softly. "Just like Granddad loves them."

A strange look crossed his face, as if he were struggling within himself over something. "They get in your blood, Kristy. Like gold. And you keep searching and digging and looking for the perfect one, which you never find, because in some way they're all perfect."

Her breathing felt ragged—it was as if he had captured all the air, just as the crystal had captured the rainbow. "That's what I felt yesterday, digging with Arvin and Wesley. I could have stayed there all day, all week, digging."

His finger traced a line down her face, along the sensitive skin beneath her jaw and came to rest in the hollow of her throat. "But could you stay for years, Kristy? Does the crystal fire burn that brightly in your blood?"

"Yes, I think it does." Except it wasn't crystal fire burning in her blood right now. Her skin felt hot where he touched her, and she saw desire burning brightly in his eyes, matching her own. She knew she should walk away from him. Before it was too late. Instead she put her hand on his chest and felt the beat of his heart, strong and even. "I have a feeling about the crystals, Mike, a feeling I've never had about anything else." She wanted him to understand, wanted him to lessen that iron control he maintained, let her see if the man she thought about was hiding in there.

He seemed to shake himself, then stepped away from her. "So. You think you've got the price thing under control?" he asked in a voice struggling for control.

She nodded, still caught up in his closeness and his talk of rainbows. "I could probably find us something to eat."

"Thanks, but I have work to do. See you tomorrow, Kristy."

He moved away. She was left holding the empty crystal and the memory of his touch. She heaved a mighty sigh and started toward the house. At that moment Mercury bounded out of the woods and almost knocked her down. He was covered with dried mud, and some really *awful* smell mixed with the remnants of the Giorgio bath gel. He looked ever so pleased with himself, but he smelled as if something large and unnamed had died behind that perfume counter at Dillard's.

"If you think you're going in the house, fella, you have another think coming. Good grief, baths are good for you, you stupid dog." The dog sat and whined and looked pitiful. "Pitiful looks will get you nowhere, Merc. You are eating outside, sleeping outside and doing whatever else it is you do outside."

She went into the house, clutching her rainbow crystal and trying very hard to remember why she had despised Mike Ferguson when she was twelve. Or even why she'd been so mad at him today. *You're falling in love with him,* a little voice nagged. "Ridiculous," she said aloud and told herself she was just curious about Mike, rather than fascinated and attracted to him.

Just before dark, two young men came to the house. They wanted to sell her some crystals, said they'd been selling to Virgil for years. She had no intention of buying, but she looked at their wares.

"Very nice," she said as they unwrapped some large points and exquisite clusters. "Where'd they come from?"

The men hemmed and hawed. "Over 'round Jessieville," one said.

"Uh, Granddad will be back in a day or two," she said. "Maybe you could check back?"

"Sure. You mind if we go out back? See what Virgil's gettin' outta his mine?"

"I guess not." She followed them and watched as they looked around and touched several of the better clusters.

After they left, Kristy remembered that the men hadn't bothered to introduce themselves.

CHAPTER SEVEN

BY THE NEXT MORNING Kristy had worked herself into a swivet about how cleverly Mike had handled her yesterday. He had accused her of abandoning her grandfather for all those years. He had concocted an outrageous shaggy, dog story about Mercury which not even a two-year-old would swallow. And last, but certainly not least, he had charmed away her anger and questions with his love of crystals and his tales of rainbows. To top it off, she had spent half the night dreaming about wandering through the woods with him, digging for the perfect crystal. Except they hadn't spent all the time digging crystals...and in the dream she had fallen head over heels in love with him. And he had fallen in love with her. Good grief, she thought, not even a Gemini was flighty enough to fall in love with a man whose only interest in a woman was to see her disappear.

By the time she finished a second cup of coffee, she was lecturing Mercury ruthlessly about the insensitivity of males in general and one Mike Ferguson in particular. Her harangue covered everything from lack of trust to chauvinism to Mercury's ungratefulness over one stupid bath and his inability to find his master. Mercury lay with his head on his great paws and kept his counsel.

She had just finished hosing down a particularly dirty table of rocks and telling Mercury what she thought of men who treated grown women like twits, when she sensed Mike's presence. Right behind her. She dropped the hose and whirled around, ready to do battle. But he stood there, hands on his hips. He wasn't quite smiling, but at least he wasn't frowning, and there was no anger in those gorgeous blue eyes this morning. Her lecture melted along with a little bit of heart.

"I heard from Virgil," he said matter-of-factly. "Well, sort of anyway."

"When?"

"Last night. A logger called me. Said he'd talked to Virgil. Virgil said to tell me not worry about him, that he was having a fine time."

"Where is he?"

"Over around Jessieville."

Was Mike telling the truth? "Isn't that a little too convenient? After my ultimatum yesterday?"

"You don't believe me?"

"I don't know." She felt the blood rush to her face as she stared at him across the few feet separating them. In the morning air she could smell the clean sharp scent of shampoo in his hair. She tried to summon her anger back. "I want to know what Chester and Virgil found during the war and if it has anything to do with where Granddad is."

He seemed to consider her for a moment, and then he spoke. "Most of the oldtimers dug crystals for the Army during World War II. For crystal radios and later for radar. The army brought in gold miners from California, and they tunneled all over these mountains until the local boys convinced them tunnels wasn't the way to dig crystals."

He made it sound almost as boring as the government bulletin had made it sound. "That's very interesting history, Mike, but it doesn't answer the question."

He turned and started for his truck, and for a minute she thought he was just going to drive off without another word. Halfway to the truck, he turned toward her, hands in his hip pockets. "Why are you so interested in the possibility that Virgil has a fortune in specimen crystals cached away somewhere?"

The implication was clear, not from the words, but from his tone, his stance, his frown. It hurt more than anything he could have said, anything he *had* said. She was speechless for a moment, but when she finally spoke, she chose her words very carefully. "Is that why you're protecting him?"

"Do you think he needs protecting?"

"I'm not even going to dignify that with an answer, except to assure you that I could care less whether Granddad's got ten fortunes or not a penny. I am here because I'm worried about my grandfather, and because I want to see him. Period." She decided to change directions in conversation before he could respond. "And if I've heard the story about the lost crystals, I think it's safe to assume that practically everyone in three counties has heard it. Dammit, you may think the whole world is like Mount Ida, but let me tell you, I live in a world where people get killed every day for a whole lot less than a fortune." They stared at each other across the yard for what seemed like an eternity. "Now is the story true or isn't it?"

He chewed his lip and stared off into the pine woods. "Legend has it that all the men who dug for the army kept back the best specimen crystals. The big clear stuff.

Legend also has it that some of them buried their caches for hard times."

"Is that what Granddad did? Is that what he's out looking for?"

"Hard times rolled around as soon as the war was over."

As usual, he had sidestepped the question. "Well, suppose the legend isn't a legend."

He shook his head and waved toward the house. "Surely you've noticed Virgil is not a millionaire. Kristy, you think I wouldn't know if Virgil had museum quality crystals stashed around here?"

"Oh, no, I'm sure you would know. I'm sure you'd know all about what Granddad has or doesn't have. I'm also sure you would do everything in your power to get rid of me before he finds them, for some obscure reason known only to you. I repeat, I don't need anything my grandfather has. Except his love," she said more sharply than she'd intended.

"It would be better if you didn't spread the legends any further than they've already spread. As you say, there are some not very nice people in the world." He turned and started toward his truck again.

She had already dismissed his taunts and turned her mind to the problem of the lost crystals. "The only thing I can't figure out is why Granddad wouldn't be able to find them again. Of course," she mused, "with all these pine trees planted like grass, I suppose the hillsides all look the same now. But—wait a minute. What are you doing here now?" she called after him.

He leaned against the truck. "I was going to take you to the mountains this morning."

She thought he sounded more subdued than she'd ever imagined he could be. "So, what changed your mind?"

He opened the door of the truck, looked at her. "I don't suppose you have any hiking boots."

She looked at her feet as if she'd never seen them before. "What do hiking boots have to do with this discussion?"

"Nothing, I guess. I wanted to look at some parcels of land I might bid on."

Halfway to the truck it occurred to her that he was probably taking her to the mountains to kill and bury her. "Why do you want me to go?" she asked suspiciously, standing still.

"I thought you might be interested, that's all."

When she refused to budge, the ghosty smile she had seen so often on Mike slowly gave way to a sheepish grin, then to a broad smile. "I might tell you some secrets."

It was the first time she had seen him really smile, and it took her breath away. It was every bit as dazzling as she had known it would be, and it changed him from a brooding, angry man to a gorgeous, charming storybook prince. Kristy took a deep breath. "That's blackmail."

"Maybe."

"I have work to do."

"It can wait." When she hesitated, he said, "People who run mines have to look at potential mining sites."

She did not for one minute believe that he was serious about teaching her the mining business. He had some other agenda. But she would go, because she wanted to know just what that agenda might be, and because it would be a good chance to interrogate him about the buried crystals and Virgil and whatever else she could think of. For some reason, he seemed more off guard and talkative than usual. And she would go because she couldn't imagine not going.

"If we're going anywhere Reebok shoes can't go," she said with a flip of her head, "I'm not interested."

They stopped at a country store on their way out of town, and Mike filled a cooler with cold drinks and cookies and sandwich meat and a loaf of soft, squishy white bread.

Kristy watched him add ice. "I cannot believe you eat such awful food. And so much of it."

"White bread is a mark of success in these parts."

"Success?"

"That's right. Last year one of my workers told me his wife had left him. Told me he couldn't understand why that woman would run off. Said, 'Mike I don't know what that woman wants from me. Why, I've fed her white bread for thirty years and that ought to be good enough for any woman.'"

In spite of herself, Kristy burst out laughing. "You made that up."

He drew his finger in a large X across his chest. "Cross my heart, it's the truth. He thought the white bread was much more important than his prodigious consumption of alcohol."

By now they were well south of Mount Ida. Mike turned off the highway and followed what was little more than a goat trail deep into the pine woods, climbing steadily. Kristy rolled down the window and breathed in the thick smell of pine and humus. They were in an area of older pine trees, not the young ones that all looked the same size.

"Why hasn't this been cut?"

"Part of it is privately owned, part of it is in the pro-posed wilderness area."

"You mean they'd let you doze and mine in here?"

"Not this part. We're just going through it."

She leaned against the door to get the full impact of the piney smell. "This area must have been breathtak-ing before the paper companies got here."

"It was. Maybe it will be again. There's lots of op-position to the clear-cut policy of the forestry service. But there are a lot of jobs involved, too. It's one of those damned if you do, damned if you don't, situa-tions."

Then they were out of the deep pines and into an area that had been cut and replanted. Mike stopped the truck at the top of a small rise. He shouldered a shovel and digging fork. "See that ridge over there?"

Kristy looked where he pointed. They were facing a steep ravine, which apparently he planned to go down, then back up the other side. Beyond the ridge he pointed to, the Ouachita mountains marched toward Oklahoma, the closer peaks a deep, piney green, the further ones a deep blue green, the farthest peaks a lovely faded blue in the late morning haze. "I would love to live right on this spot and look out every morn-ing on those mountains," she said quietly.

"I don't think the forestry boys would let you," he said in a strange voice. "But there are other places as beautiful. A lot of people come here, taken by the beauty, then they find out they can't handle the isola-tion. They go back to civilization."

"But you can always visit a city if you need that."

"Maybe. I'm just telling you what happens." He pointed again. "We're going to that ridge."

His voice brought her back. "You're kidding."

"Nope."

He led the way, stopping occasionally to dig a hole and examine the soil. Kristy noted that he always carefully filled it back in and tamped the soil down.

When they finally struggled up the other side of the ravine, he stood for a long time, looking at the terrain and the rock formations. Then he began to dig with the shovel.

Kristy took the digging fork and went a little way off and began to dig her own hole. Within minutes, she had found three tiny crystal points. "Look at these."

He came over and rubbed the dirt off them and examined them carefully.

"So? How are they?"

"Not bad, but if there's a good vein, it's probably fifty, seventy feet down."

"How do you know that?" she asked suspiciously.

"It just doesn't feel right."

"Feel right? That doesn't sound very scientific."

He laughed. "I guess it doesn't, but that's as close as I can come to an explanation. Virgil and Chester used to tell me they could smell a vein. I can't tell you how many hours I spent in these woods sniffing away, waiting for the right smell to overwhelm me."

"And it never did?"

"It never did. I'm still not as good as Granddad was, but I can tell a lot from the soil and the rock formations." He looked out over the ravine. "Did they ever bring you up here when you were a kid?"

"I don't think so. I don't recognize anything. Of course, I guess it's all changed since then." She looked south. "That bluff looks kind of familiar. There was a bluff and a creek I remember. I don't know. I might recognize some of the places if I saw them again."

He shouldered the shovel again. "Well, let's go eat a bite, then try the bluff."

They sat on the tailgate of the truck and ate gummy sandwiches. Kristy thought they tasted wonderful. A squirrel came to sample a bread crust and scold for more. Insects buzzed, and Kristy felt all the tension of the past few days drain away. She took her cola and nestled down on the thick carpet of needles at the base of an old pine, which for some reason had been spared the ax. The morning had passed, and she hadn't asked him one question about Virgil's disappearance, let alone interrogated him. She was too content to listen to his stories and to be with him. She gazed at the mountains. "This is a hard country to make a living in, isn't it?"

"That it is. Most of the ground is too poor for farming. Except for growing pine trees. People have spent their lives eking out a living in these mountains. Until a couple of years ago, the war was the best time of their lives. They made good money, bought land and built their homes. Then there were the long, lean years, when there wasn't any market for their rocks." He stretched out on the tailgate, his weight on his elbow. "Then quartz crystals swept the electronics industry, and there was a market again. The New Age craze has put everyone back in full swing again. It's been good for the area."

She wanted to know all there was to know about crystals. "I never understood how they work."

"They oscillate at very precise frequencies. They're what makes your quartz watch keep accurate time."

Kristy frowned. "I still don't understand it.'

"It's magic. They also used quartz for bomb sights. It filters out the ultraviolet end of the spectrum."

When she looked up, he was watching her with an intensity that made her uncomfortable. She squirmed deeper into the pine needles. "Whatever *that* means."

"Chester always said that if he had all the rocks he sold for bomb sights during the war, he'd be a rich man. They only took the finest, clearest stuff for that."

She leaned her head against the tree and closed her eyes. "I don't care about watches and VCRs and bomb sights. I want to find the biggest, most beautiful crystal that the world has ever seen."

"You and half the world, Kristy," he said softly.

"So why are you tending Virgil's mine instead of your own?"

He shrugged. "I have good people working for me. Virgil needed some help."

She could tell that he had no intention of discussing the mine any further, but he seemed more open to talk than usual, so she decided to venture into history. "Mike, what happened between Daddy and Virgil?"

"Ask Garrett."

She knew from the change in his voice that she had hit a nerve. "End of discussion?"

"End of discussion." He stood up and began packing the ice chest again. "Let's try the bluff. Sure you can make it?"

"Yeah, I can make it, Mike." It occurred to her that this whole trip might be some kind of test. She had to scramble to keep up with him on the long trek to the bluff, but she kept up and refused to let him help her over any of the rough places. When they got there, she remembered it from her youth because of the huge fossil rock that made up part of the rock formation. A creek meandered slowly at its base. Mike dug in silence, and she sensed that he was angry with her, or with himself or something. All that her attempts at conversation brought were grunts and flying dirt from his shovel. Lunch had been so much fun, but now he was in one of those moods again. Finally they shouldered their tools and started back to the truck.

Mike loaded the tools, then rested his elbows on the pickup and looked at her across the truck bed. "Look, I put some money in Virgil's mine because it's an investment. I help him when he needs help, but I don't interfere in his business."

"Meaning I should do the same?"

"I didn't say that. Virgil and I just have a way of getting along. Maybe it's strange to other people, but it works for us. When my dad ran off, Chester practically raised me, but he had a lot of help from Virgil. Virgil seemed to know more about kids than Granddad."

"I don't think my father would agree with that," Kristy replied and got into the truck.

"No, I guess he wouldn't." He got in the truck and sat staring out the windshield, his hands gripping the steering wheel. "It almost killed Virgil when Garrett left that summer and Virgil knew he wasn't coming back."

She heard the emotion in his voice. "It must have been a terrible argument," she said softly, hoping he would continue.

His bitter laughter was too loud in the closeness of the cab. "There wasn't *any* argument. Not that time. Garrett left in the night. He couldn't even face Virgil and tell him why."

Kristy's hand went to her mouth to smother the sound struggling for release. "Oh, Mike, no wonder he's—"

"It's all ancient history." He reached in the grocery sack. "Want a Twinkie treat?"

Kristy was still reeling from the image of her father stealing away in the night, unable to face Virgil's disappointment and perhaps his anger. "What?"

"A Twinkie cake."

She could tell from the tension in his face and his body that he had told her something he had never meant to, and he was in some way pleading with her to not pursue the topic. She struggled within herself. Should she ask for more information or drop it and hope he would tell her more later. Her instincts said he needed time. She smiled to let him know she had all the time in the world. "You eat Twinkies?"

"Everyone eats Twinkies."

"Nobody I know over twelve."

"Then you don't know many people."

"They're sugar and chemicals."

"They're good." He ate half of one in one bite and handed her the other half.

In truth, Kristy had never eaten a Twinkie treat. Her mother equated them to poison and intimated that dire things happened to people who ate foods of that nature. She cautiously took a great bite and smiled. "They're gooey."

"That's what makes them so great."

They rode home in a companionable silence. Kristy pointed to things and asked questions about the area, but her mind was busy with what he had said. She knew that her father's leaving was only half the story, that the months and years that followed were the rest of it. They must have been terrible years for Virgil if Mike, an impressionable boy at the time, had been so affected. She knew now why Mike had been so desperate to get rid of her, and it made her love him a little more. She would have to prove to him that this time it would be different.

When he pulled into the driveway and killed the engine, she was reluctant for the day to end. "Want some coffee?"

"I'd better take a rain check. I need to get some bids ready."

She knew they were on shaky ground again, but he had been strangely pleasant most of the day, so she thought she might wander onto the eggshells again and see what happened. "Mr. Eldridge mentioned the other day that Granddad wanted to do some bids. You want me to go to town to sign them?"

"I'll take care of it."

"Right." He might have spent the afternoon with her, but Virgil's business was still none of her business. "I was just trying to save you a trip."

"Sam doesn't always get the paperwork right these days."

"Yeah." She got out of the truck and pushed the door shut. The afternoon had been wonderful. He had talked to her, been nice, given her a Hostess Twinkie, then shut her out completely. All of which made her wonder again why he had taken her with him in the first place. He was a strange man, to say the least, but she had a feeling that if she could ever get through that defensive exterior, he would be the kind of man dreams are made of. She sighed and thought she had best get her mind on safer matters.

She retired to the porch with a peanut butter sandwich—on whole wheat bread—and her weekly astrological chart. It was high time she got her life organized and knew what she was dealing with.

Before she went to bed, she called her father to get his side of the story. She loved her father and knew that if he'd left in the night, he'd done it because he'd felt he had to. But when he answered, she realized it was not something they could handle over the phone. So she just told him that Virgil was still missing, that she had everything under control and that the crystal business was booming. She did not tell him about all the crazy people running around the countryside with dynamite. Or that she would stay in Mount Ida forever if Mike wanted her to, which was about as likely as Mercury flying to the moon.

CHAPTER EIGHT

Two DAYS had passed since the trip to the mountains. Mike brought a load of rocks each morning, Kristy cleaned and cooked them. He was pleasant but distant, as if watching and waiting for her to demand more answers about Virgil. She had to bite her tongue to keep from doing exactly that, but bite it she did, determined that she would quietly go about her work and let him make the first move.

She lifted a rack of crystals out of the tank and examined the contents in the rosy light of dawn. They looked clean and bright. She hosed them off and began to sort them, trying to remember everything Mike had told her about color and clarity and chipped points and form. She carefully examined each point and cluster, then put them in one of three racks. Really good ones, not so good ones and the ones she didn't think she could possibly bear to sell. When the sun touched them, they sparkled and glittered, and Kristy thought they were the most beautiful things she had ever seen.

When she got them sorted, she noticed with a sinking feeling that most of the crystals lay in the rack she had set aside for herself. She sorted them again and managed to part with three more small clusters. She wondered if she could sort them at night ... by feel.

She began going through them again, ruthlessly, lecturing herself sternly about sound business practices.

After all, where would she put all those crystals? And if she stayed here long enough, she would have a veritable mountain of "favorite" crystals. She held one particularly nice double-terminator for a moment, then stuck it in her pocket. Everyone needed a pocket crystal.

She didn't even look up from her work until Mercury howled and she realized that John Graves had driven up. He got out of the truck and walked toward her, looking, she thought, a bit grim for such a beautiful morning. He carried something wrapped in newspapers. She smiled and waved.

"I was hoping to catch Mike here."

"Haven't seen him this morning. Can I help you?"

He laid his package on one of the wire tables and began to unwrap it. Kristy gasped when she saw it. It was a single point. A foot long, as big as her arm, as clear as glass. She touched the crystal gently, ran her fingers up and down its length. It was as smooth as glass, with none of the tiny ridges so characteristic of the ones she'd been cleaning. Mike had talked about crystals like this one.

"It's gorgeous," she whispered. "Where on earth did you find it?"

"Couple of boys were showing it around over near Pencil Bluff. They took off in kind of a hurry when they saw me. Must have dropped it. I think they're the same ones that have been doing a little midnight mining here and there."

She stared at the point, unable to think of anything except the excitement of finding one like that. Her crystal fever jumped another notch.

"I was hoping to get Mike's opinion on where it came from. It doesn't look like anything being mined now."

"Oh?" she murmured, still staring.

"Looks like it might have come from the old Coleman mine, except they've got fences and pretty tight security over there. Might even be from the McEarl mine." He wrapped the crystal again, and Kristy felt as if the sun had disappeared.

"I guess Mike's at the mine," she said.

John tipped his hat. "I'll try to catch him there. By the way, the rangers are keeping an eye out for Virgil."

"I can't imagine why someone hasn't run across him." She could very well imagine a reason, but she refused to dwell on it.

"A man who doesn't want to be found could stay lost forever in these mountains, ma'am. Particularly a man who knows them as well as Virgil. That's assuming Virgil doesn't want to be found."

She noticed that he carefully avoided any reference to how easy it would be to hide a body in these mountains. "I just wish he'd come back."

"Yes, ma'am." As the forestry man started toward his truck, Mike drove in.

"John, how are you?"

"Okay. You?"

Graves nodded and began to unwrap the crystal on the hood of his truck. Kristy watched Mike carefully, waiting to see his delight at such a magnificent specimen. Instead she saw a frown begin, and recognition flashed in his eyes for a brief instant. He chewed his lip as Graves told the story of how he came by the crystal. Mike's fingers drummed a tense rhythm on the hood of the truck.

"The McEarl mine?" Graves asked.

Mike rubbed his chin and glanced at Kristy. "No. It likely came from a pocket we hit at Virgil's mine a few weeks ago." Graves frowned. "We just got a few."

Kristy could feel the tension between the two men and wondered what was going on. She walked closer.

Graves carefully wrapped the crystal. "If this rock came from Virgil's mine, it was planted there. You know, and I know, there aren't any rocks like this in that mine."

"I'm in that mine every day, John. We had a theft a couple of weeks ago. That rock was in the batch."

The forestry man started to say something then seemed to change his mind. "I guess you know there's a big outfit from Santa Fe bidding on parcels and trying to buy some established mines. They don't seem to know diddly-squat about mining, but they sure seem to have a bottomless checkbook."

"Yeah, they talked to me. You think they have some front men doing a little midnight sampling?"

Graves shrugged. "Or they may be hiring some of the local boys to do it for them. If the boys who had this rock are who I think they are, they haven't got sense enough to plan a robbery—they just do what they're told. I figure they stole this from whoever hired them."

"So if you know who they are, why don't you bring them in?"

"They were clean the one time I stopped them. I need to catch them with something."

Mike quickly started toward his truck. "I've got some bids in the truck, John. You want to take them now?" The two men walked to Mike's pickup. Out of earshot, Kristy noticed.

She sorted rocks and listened but only caught a few words. In the next few minutes, though, it became obvious that the two men were arguing. Mike kept explaining something, and Graves kept shaking his head. She heard Virgil's name several times and thought she heard "that girl" once. The longer they argued, the madder she got. More secrets. Mike was no doubt telling the forestry man everything he refused to tell her.

When Graves drove off, Mike started pacing between his truck and the tanks like some sort of caged animal.

"More secrets, Mike?" she asked, sarcasm dripping from her voice as she forgot about all her vows of silence. "Things I don't need to know about?"

"What?" He stared at her as if he'd never seen her before.

"That crystal has something to do with Granddad, doesn't it?" When Mike didn't answer, cold fear touched her. "What happened, Mike? Is that one of the crystals that—" Suddenly, the cocoon of confidence that Mike had wrapped her in with his assurances ripped apart. Her comforting theory that Mike knew where Virgil was and simply wasn't telling her shattered like a fragile crystal dropped in a boiling tank. "Damn it, Mike, talk to me."

"It's nothing important. John's wrong. Come on, I need you at the mine today."

Kristy stared at him as if he had taken leave of his senses. "Forget the mine, Mike. I want to know what you and John Graves were arguing about." He stopped pacing and took several breaths. She could see him fighting for control. Finally he smiled, but the smile was tight and controlled.

He laid his hands on her shoulders. "Kristy, this doesn't have anything to do with Virgil. Now that crystal probably came out of a private collection. Which means the thieves could hit this place. There's nothing that valuable here, but they might not know that. I'd feel safer if you were at the mine."

She was so touched by his concern for her safety, it wiped away the thoughts she had been entertaining—of screaming at him, demanding he tell her something, and thoughts of going directly to the sheriff and demanding an all-out search be launched. "But—"

"I thought you wanted to learn all about mining. Come on, I'm running late."

It was more like an order than an invitation. She started to argue, but one look at his face and the argument died in her throat. She didn't have any idea what was going on, but for some reason that beautiful crystal had put Mike into a Class A swivet, and she was sure the crystal had something to do with Virgil. She quickly decided she would have a better chance of finding the truth at the mine than stewing around at the house. "Well, what are you waiting for?" she asked, her voice as hard as his.

He drove in silence, as if he were in a time trial for the Indy-500. Every time she glanced at him, his face was more of a thundercloud than the last time, so she, too, rode in silence. Perhaps Arvin and Wesley would know something. She wanted to trust Mike, wanted to believe he had everything under control, wanted to believe Virgil was safe, because the other options were too awful to even consider.

Minutes later, they were in the bottom of the pit. She saw Arvin and Wesley wrapping crystals from a newly dozed area, and Mike was talking to his foreman.

When she looked again, Mike was gone. She wanted to borrow a car and go after him, but she knew she would never catch him. She walked over to Arvin and

Wesley, determined to throw herself into the digging so that she wouldn't think about anything else.

Before the morning was over, she was digging in her own pocket of crystals. The two men hovered and showed her how to get under the clusters with the bar and pry so that she didn't damage the points. Arvin did all the talking. Wesley showed her how to do things and smiled, but hardly said a word. She didn't think she had ever known a young man so shy. They showed her how to feel the clay for points, how to decide whether they were good enough to wrap or too broken to keep. She found one delicate cluster bristling with tiny points that she knew she couldn't part with. The men chuckled at her enthusiasm and told her tales of other digs, other mines, other times. "Why do you do it, Arvin?" she asked. Mike had told her his reasons, but she wanted another opinion.

"Kinda gets in your blood," Arvin said. "I guess we'd be diggin' these rocks even if we wasn't gettin' paid."

It was the same thing Mike had said.

She questioned Arvin from time to time about Virgil and Mike and other things. All Arvin would say was, "If Mike says it, you can take it to the bank." Whatever *that* was supposed to mean. "Did you work with Daddy, Arvin?" she asked.

"Surely did. We loved that boy like one of our own. Went real hard on Virgil when he left."

"So I've heard. Granddad got sick, didn't he?" She was fishing, but she wanted information.

"Real hard it was for Virgil. Now see this pocket over here? We're gonna have to dig around it a bit." Kristy noted that the men of Mount Ida were masters at secrets and changing the subject.

But before the morning was over their contagion had spread to her and true crystal fever had seeped into her bloodstream. She realized with a bit of a shock that these men—and Mike—*would* be out in the woods digging for rocks even if they couldn't sell them. They would do whatever was required to support their families, but they would dig. They couldn't put it into words, but it was there, as clear as the crystals they dug. Her peers at school talked of corporate ladders, tenure tracks, perks and retirement plans. These men talked of doing what they loved. They took the *real* jobs when times were hard, but they still dug crystals. It was who they were, it was what they did.

Her heart beat faster, and Kristy knew she wanted to be a part of it all. These beautiful bits of rock, formed by fire and water millions of years ago, were the thing she had searched for. The thing she could devote her life to.

When they broke for lunch, Mike was still gone. "Do you know when Mike will be back?" she asked Arvin. "I still have a lot of work to do at the house."

"Ain't no tellin', ma'am. Prob'ly over to his place seein' about things."

"Oh." Kristy realized she had no idea what sort of operation Mike had. She had assumed it must be a fairly small one since he had time to help Virgil. Yet, he had extra money to put into this mine. The idleness of the lunch break gave her time to start worrying and stewing again, so she decided it was time she found out a bit more about Mike Ferguson and his business. It might give her a better idea of how much faith to put in his ideas about mining and Virgil and...other things.

"Arvin, could I borrow your car for a little while? I need to run a few errands."

The old man dug in his pocket for keys. "You bet. It's the fifty-six Ford pickup." When she nonchalantly asked Arvin where Mike's place was, he told her.

Since none of the heavy equipment seemed to be running, Kristy walked out of the pit. She was gasping for air when she reached the top. She had no idea what a fifty-six Ford pickup looked like, only that it was bound to look different from everything else.

When she spotted the vehicle, she laughed. It was midnight blue with custom chrome and totally unlike anything she would imagine Arvin driving. When she climbed in, the cab looked big enough for a party, and the steering wheel was twice the size of her car's. But the engine purred quietly, and the truck even had an automatic transmission. She had to sit on the edge of the seat to reach the pedals.

She went through Mount Ida and turned on 270. Just past the intersection, she almost ran the truck off the road at the sight that greeted her. On her right sat a beautiful cedar and stone building and a sign that read Ferguson Mine Retail Shop. Across the highway, a chain link fence enclosed a huge metal building. A sign said Ferguson Mining Co. Wholesale Only. The fenced yard bristled with crystals, clusters ranging from the size of a bushel basket to that of a pickup truck bed. Row after row of wire tables filled with single points and smaller clusters sparkled in the sun.

Kristy pulled into the retail shop parking lot and stared. She had assumed Mike was a successful businessman, but this went beyond plain old successful. He must be *wildly* successful. Which made her more than a bit suspicious about his "I dig them because I love them" line. It might be true for Arvin and Wesley and Virgil, but obviously Mike made a lot of money dig-

ging crystals. She got out of the truck and ducked into
the retail shop. The walls were lined with lighted glass
shelves. There were crystals on light boxes, there were
crystals on funny pedestals where the light changed
from red to blue to green, transforming the points into
a fairyland of shape and color. There were exquisite
crystal balls, and crystals in locked cases with two-
thousand-dollar price tags.

Kristy was overwhelmed by the beauty and the prices
and the inventory. The crystals she had been cleaning
wouldn't even get in the front door of this shop. Why
was Mike Ferguson so busy with Virgil's mine when he
had access to quartz of this quality? Was he *that* loyal
to Virgil? In her world, wildly successful young men did
not ignore their own businesses to help someone else. It
made Mike too good to be true.

She smiled at the young woman who had been trail-
ing her around the shop and left, then herded the old
truck across the highway and marched into the wholesale building. The entire center of the building was open
and one wall was lined with long, metal gas-fired
cleaning tanks that made Virgil's backyard operation
look like something out of the stone age. To her right
was a door marked Office, to her left, Display Room.
Before she could make up her mind which to try, an
older woman came out of the office.

"May I help you?" The woman looked at Kristy's
clay-covered clothes and smiled. "Been digging, I see.
Find anything good?"

Kristy shrugged. "I just wanted to look around."

"Well, this is wholesale only. The retail shop is across
the street."

Kristy smiled, straightened herself and brushed clay
from her face. What would her mother do in a situa-

tion like this? Bull right ahead, that's what. "Oh, I know. That's why I'm here. I'm Penny Jackson. From the coast, you know." She waved in the general direction of what she hoped was west.

"Yes?"

"Well, a friend of mine in Frisco said that there was simply no other place in the world to buy crystals except from you people."

"That's very nice," the woman said, obviously still not convinced she was a real buyer.

"Well, I'd like to see what you have. My retail shops are simply down to the bone."

"Of course." The woman produced a key and unlocked the display room door. The room apparently had no windows, and they stepped into murky darkness. When the woman flipped a light switch, Kristy gasped. Nothing she had seen at Virgil's or the mine or anywhere else prepared her for the exquisite collection of crystals that rested on velvet-covered tables and glittered in glass cabinets around the walls. "Oh, they're lovely," she whispered and made a beeline for a cluster the size of a turkey platter with a dozen or more clear, smooth points ranging up to a foot in height. A discreet price tag lay beside it. $10,000.

"That's my favorite one, too. It's from near the old Coleman mine." When Kristy didn't respond, the woman continued. "You understand we can make some adjustment on the price when your order gets above a hundred thousand."

"A hundred thousand," Kristy sputtered. "Of course." She felt like a kid in a candy store. She wanted to see them all, touch them all. Take them all home. She moved to the shelves. There were clusters of points so small she could hold them in the palm of her hand, the crystals growing from them tiny and perfect and jewel-like. In the middle of the shelf was a formation unlike anything she had ever seen or imagined. It was like a sea urchin, except the spines were all long, clear double-terminators. The cluster had all the beauty and form and elegance of a sculpted piece of art, except Kristy knew it had come out of the ground in just that shape. And she knew she had to have it.

"I want that one." She would sell the BMW and buy a truck. She would rob a bank. She would call her father for operating capital.

"Of course. Did you have any idea how much you wanted to spend?"

Wanted or could? "Oh, perhaps a hundred thousand or so. How much is this one?"

"I'm afraid Mr. Ferguson will have to price that one. It would be by weight."

At that moment, she heard Mike's voice. "Madge, I'm back."

"In here."

Kristy desperately looked around for a place to hide and cursed the fact that there were no windows for escape. She could do a window-crashing Superman exit. She took refuge in the corner with her back to the door and squatted down as if admiring something on the lowest shelf. When she sneaked a look under the tables, she saw advancing boots and jeans.

"I've got to go back out to the mine and pick up the prodigal granddaughter. Maybe a full day in the mine will convince her she should go home."

"From what you've told me, work doesn't faze her one bit. Don't be so hard on her, Mike. She must be a wreck about Virgil."

"Right, Madge. So why wasn't she a wreck all those years when he was all alone."

"She might have reasons you know nothing about, Michael, and she's at his place now. So you be nice."

"You, dear Madge, don't have to put up with her."

The woman laughed. "I haven't seen you this worked up in years, Mike. I think you like that girl more than you want to admit."

"You think wrong, Madge."

Kristy's face burned with embarrassment and something else. Darn him anyway.

"Oh, wait, Mike," Madge called. "You need to price the double-terminator piece."

Kristy heard the steps coming closer and wanted to crawl under a nearby table. All of the feet stopped very close to her. She kept staring at the shelf of rocks.

"Miss Jackson? This is Mr. Ferguson. Miss Jackson is from the coast. She's interested in a large order, and she definitely wants the double-terminator piece."

Suddenly he was looming over her, hands on his hips. "Thank you, Madge, I'll take care of it. Could you check on those invoices we talked about this morning?"

Kristy could hear the mixture of amusement and anger in his voice. She pointed to a small crystal ball. "Did you make this or did it come this way?" She felt his hand on her arm, pulling her up, whirling her around. "By the way, where have you been all day?" She had little hope that he would tell her, but she thought she should take the offensive.

"Let me help you with your selections, Ms. Jackson. A large order? Hundred thousand? Two?"

Kristy shrugged him off and tried to back away from him, but she ended up in a corner with Mike glaring at her. "Well, I was curious. And that lady wasn't going to let me in until I promised to buy legions of your crystals."

"You could have just asked me." He brushed a strand of hair away from her face. "I would have been glad to show you my operation."

He smelled of piney woods and rich dirt and sweat, and she felt her heart beat a little faster. "Well I assumed it was probably a secret. Buried in the bowels of some mountain. Everything else around here seems to be a secret." He rubbed a spot of dirt from her nose, and his touch felt like a white-hot laser. His eyes bored into her very soul. She brushed his hand away. "And you could have told me you were rich."

"What does rich have to do with anything?"

"I don't know," she said crossly, trying to break the spell his eyes were casting. She ducked under his arm and walked between the tables, stopping occasionally to touch an especially beautiful crystal point. He followed on her heels.

"Well, I'm waiting."

She turned to face him. "Why are you messing with that old mine when you obviously have a better one? I mean things like this didn't come from any old abandoned mine."

He traced a finger down her cheek. "It all has to do with an old man and his dreams, Kristy. You wouldn't understand."

She brushed his finger away and took a step backward. She couldn't think with him looming about, touching her, distracting her, which she was sure he was doing on purpose. "Why don't you try me?"

He smiled and straightened her collar. "Maybe if you eavesdrop enough, you'll figure it out."

She resumed her stroll among the tables. "I was not eavesdropping. I was minding my own business."

"Under false pretences, I might add."

She pointed to the double-terminator formation. "I was not. I want that one."

"That one sells by the gram. I'd have to weigh it, but I'm guessing it would cost fifteen hundred. Give or take a hundred."

She gulped. "I don't care."

"We don't sell singles. We do wholesale."

"So carry it across the street and I'll buy it there."

"Ah, but it would be three thousand over there."

"That's absurd."

"That's cash flow and turnaround and overhead."

"Keep it, then. I'll go find one by myself." She marched out of the building and climbed into the truck. She heard Mike explaining to Madge that Ms. Jackson had miraculously become Ms. Cunningham while she was in the display room.

On her way back to the mine, Kristy realized that although Mike had been annoyed with her—as usual—he had relaxed from the steel-sprung Mike who had unceremoniously dumped her at the mine that morning. And he was going out of his way to distract her and enjoying the heck out of her turning to silly putty every time he turned on the charm. She decided he was the most moody, self-centered, fascinating, awful man she had ever known. Bordering on schizophrenic.

"I despise that man," she said to the fuzzy monkey hanging from the rearview mirror. *Or you love him,* a little voice nagged for the umpteenth time. She almost wrecked the truck when that thought hit her. She pulled into a small café to calm down before returning to the mine. She ordered a sandwich and strong coffee, hoping to calm her nervous stomach and shaking hands. She wasn't in love, she was just intrigued, curious, fascinated, none of which had anything to do with love.

When she reached the mine, she noticed Mike's truck was there. She slipped and slid down the incline to the pit and rejoined her crew as if she had never been gone. She felt Mike watching her, but she refused to even look at him, let alone acknowledge him.

When they quit for the day, Kristy informed Mike that she was riding with Arvin. Mike informed her she was riding with him. To discuss her wholesale purchase. She fumed but finally gave in rather than create a scene.

When she got into his truck, she immediately went on the offensive. "I'll give you a check for that crystal. Surely you can break your stupid rules once and sell a single."

"I don't think so." He started down the mountain. "But I'll give it to you," he said.

Kristy sneaked a sideways glance at him, suspicious of his sudden generosity. "Why?"

"For Virgil. For your work. To remember us by."

"I haven't done that much work, and I'm not going anywhere, so I don't need any souvenirs." She rolled the window down to gulp in the fresh air, which turned out to be full of dust.

He shrugged. "Because it's mine to give."

"I won't take it. I want to buy it."

"Not for sale."

"Then forget it." She was sorely tempted by his offer, but she could only imagine what the hidden price might be if she took the lovely crystal. And it occurred to her for a brief moment that it might be worth it. Except it was probably just another tactic in his strategy to get rid of her before Virgil got back.

He shrugged again and kept his eyes on the road. "Why do you have to stub up over everything I say?"

"The same reason you stub up over everything I do."

"Want some dinner?"

"No." She gave him a suspicious sideways glance. "Why are you being so nice all of a sudden?"

"I guess I'm stuck with you for a while, so we should get to know each other all over again."

"Why don't I believe you?"

He reached over and took her hand. "Because you have a very suspicious nature."

As he squeezed and massaged her scraped hands, the warmth spread up her arm and radiated throughout her body. It would be so easy, so nice, to give in to his game, but she couldn't. Not until she had some answers, not until she knew who he was. "And you have a lot of secrets."

They pulled into the yard. Mike went out back to unload, and she stomped into the house. And stopped, her hand rising of its own accord to her mouth to stifle the scream. Furniture was overturned, cushions ripped, drawers pulled out and emptied. The house looked as if a maniac had been turned loose. She slowly backed out the door. "Mike," she whispered. "Mike!" The last was a scream.

CHAPTER NINE

MIKE COVERED the distance from the backyard almost before the cry died in her throat. "What is it?"

She pointed to the house. He stepped cautiously inside and quickly checked all the rooms, then came back and led her in, his arm around her. She leaned against him and put her arm around his waist. He pulled her closer. "It's okay, Kristy," he said softly, "they're gone."

As they stood together in the wrecked living room, Kristy felt her initial shock and fear begin to fade into anger. Not because someone had wrecked things, but that someone had violated her... privacy, her grandfather's world. "Who would do something like this?"

"I don't know, but I intend to find out." He set a chair upright and gently sat her down on it, then called the sheriff. When he finished, he sat on a footstool in front of her, one hand on her leg, the other smoothing her hair away from her face. "Are you okay?" She nodded. "We'll need to know if anything is missing."

She was aware of his gentle touch but not in the same way she had been aware of him before. She felt safe, protected. "How can I tell?" But amazingly enough, her mind was already surveying and inventorying the wreckage. About the only things that hadn't been tossed around were the crystals. A few of them lay on the floor, but the ones in the windowsill were untouched. It didn't make any sense.

"As soon as the sheriff takes a look, we'll get things straightened up again." He held her face in his hands. "Kristy, you can't stay here until we find out who did this. I have room at my place or you can go to a motel."

She heard the concern in his voice, and at some level was touched by it, but her anger overwhelmed everything else at this moment. "No. Whoever did this isn't going to scare me off."

"Kristy, this isn't a game."

"What were they looking for?"

He stood up and turned away. "I don't know. It was probably just some kids who thought Virgil had money hidden."

She jumped up. "Mike, you know darn well kids didn't do this. Kids would have taken the crystals and sold them. Now why don't you tell me what's going on around here?"

She saw his shoulders tense. "You think I know who did this and why?" His voice was as soft as silk, yet as cold as a blast of winter through the pines.

"I don't know what to think. All I know is one minute you're Dr. Jekyll, the next minute Mr. Hyde. I know you very conveniently got me out of the house today." Even as she said the words she didn't believe them, but maybe she could shock him into telling her the truth about Virgil, the mine, the lost crystals. He might not know *who* had trashed the house, but she was certain he knew *why* they did it.

When he turned to face her, his eyes reminded her of deep cold water. "You think I did this?"

She refused to back down before those icy blue eyes. "Well, you sure had the opportunity. And you sure as hell know something about Virgil. I think you've been off looking for him today. To tell him about the crystal John Graves had. And you either found Granddad and haven't bothered to tell me." She took a deep breath. "Or you *couldn't* find him, which means something's happened. Which is it, Mike?" she asked, her voice little more than a whisper.

"If you believe that, you don't know a damn thing about me, Kristy."

"Well, we finally agree on something." Before the argument could escalate, a deputy arrived. He asked questions, wrote a report and left. Kristy doubted that anything would come of it, but at least his presence defused the tension between her and Mike. When they were alone again amidst the wreckage, she didn't return to the conversation, perhaps afraid of his answer. "Mike—"

"Let's get this place cleaned up." He quickly started picking up furniture and putting it back in place.

She sighed. Obviously there would be no further discussion of anything that mattered. "I'll do it."

"It's too much. You need help."

"I do not. I am perfectly capable of cleaning up a trashed house. I've had a lot of roommates."

He put his hands on her shoulders and shook her gently. "Listen to me. I don't want anything to happen to you."

She saw the distress in his eyes, felt her heart beat faster. Had he finally accepted her? Did he feel some of the same things she felt?

"I may not approve of your being here, but I don't want you hurt."

She pulled away from him. So much for his feelings. She should have known better. "I didn't think you did, Mike. I was just looking for someone to yell at. Okay?"

"If you won't go to a motel, go home, Kristy. It would be safer for everyone until we get this thing sorted out."

She didn't even respond—she just started cleaning up. They quickly got the living room reasonably straight. When they saw that the thieves had not gotten as far as the bedrooms, Mike started on her again about leaving for the night. She refused again. "I'll be fine. Things can't be any more dangerous here than they are living in the city. Besides, Merc will no doubt show up for supper. I'll lock him in the house with me."

He gave her a hint of a smile. "If Merc is all that's between you and danger, I think you have a serious problem."

"At least he barks. Sometimes."

He quickly wrote a number on the pad by the phone. "Call me if you need me. And the only reason I'm giving in is because I assume the thieves had plenty of time here. They either found what they were looking for or they didn't. In either case, I don't think they'll be back." ~

"I'll be just fine." She could tell he was hesitant to leave. One part of her wanted him to stay, another part wanted him to leave. She didn't want to appear helpless. He had been protective and gentle as a lamb when he led her back into the ransacked living room, but the more she thought about it, the more she decided it was the way he would have treated a frightened child. She needed to prove to him—and to herself—that she was perfectly capable of taking care of herself, and that she wasn't the least bit scared. She would probably have to sit up all night to prove that, but she thought it might be worth it. Besides, she didn't really think the burglars or whatever they were would come back twice in one day.

"Okay." He wiped a smudge from her nose. "Wash your face."

She watched him drive away, her finger gently touching her nose, unwilling to wash away his touch. She knew she should pack up and go home, not because she was frightened, but because she was getting too involved with Mike. An involvement that was one-sided and would end in her getting hurt. He'd made himself all too clear. He would put up with her temporarily, protect her temporarily, because she was Virgil's granddaughter. He might even make love to her—she knew he felt something physical for her—but that too would be temporary, and she couldn't live with that. Or with the bitterness he felt toward her father.

She pushed those thoughts aside, did a little more cleaning, walked the floor, fumed at whoever had taken such liberties with her grandfather's property and listened to every little sound. She thought about calling Mr. Eldridge to tell him what had happened but decided against it. He would probably have a heart attack.

Later two customers came and she visited with them for almost an hour while they looked through the shop. They were nice young women who said they were looking for crystals because they were so beautiful. They did a lot to boost her spirits, and they bought fifty dollars' worth of crystals.

Just before dark, she heard something moving through the woods, and she grabbed up the old rifle she had found in the closet. The weapon appeared to date back to the Civil War, and she had no idea how to shoot it, but it was so...lethal looking, she decided pointing it would do the trick. She braced herself against the far wall of the living room and waited.

Mercury thundered onto the porch and scratched at the screen. She breathed a sigh of relief and went to let him in, then locked the door behind him. "It's watch-dog time tonight, Merc." He panted and made his smiling face, waiting for his food. Kristy noticed that he smelled like a mixture of wet dog and dead animal. "Good grief, Mercury, where do you find all this stuff you roll in?"

The dog lapped up his food and kept his counsel.

As she ate her nightly soup—and wished for a pizza—the phone rang. She answered it cautiously, wondering who on earth might be calling. Probably Mike to check on her.

"Kristy, you won't believe where I am." Penny sounded as if she'd just inherited an investment banking firm.

"Oh, Penny. Am I glad to hear from you. *Where* are you?"

"I'm in Dallas. I came to a banking thing, and they're having a big rock and crystal show in the convention center next to the hotel. I can't believe it. You have a whole mine full of that quartz stuff?"

"Kind of. I thought you didn't like stuff like that."

"I thought they were just rocks. You know, plain old rocks that the lunatic fringe went for. Listen, Kristy, there's a big demand in Asia for this stuff. Industrial use. I can probably set your grandfather up with a Japanese conglomerate. They do the money, your granddad sits back and collects royalties."

Kristy laughed. She could just see her roommate's mind doing cartwheels over the prospect of such a thing.

"I'll set up the marketing strategy. For a piece of the action, of course."

"Penny, hold on. We're doing mostly specimen stuff for collectors and shops. Ferguson Mines does most of the wholesale and industrial stuff."

"So talk to him. We'll take part of his market."

Kristy had a sudden, lifesize image of marching up to Mike and informing him that she and her roommate were taking over his industrial market. He would have a *stroke*. "It's not quite that simple, Penny. Is it a big show?"

"Huge. People from all over the world."

Kristy's mind began doing its own cartwheels. "Penny, are there any sellers from Arkansas?"

"Sure. I mean, I don't know. I spent most of my time talking to a couple of foreign conglomerates who want an integrated operation. From mine to finished product."

"Listen, Penny, I want you to do something. It's very important. Check and see who's selling Arkansas crystal. If you can't get their names, get descriptions. I'm particularly interested in two young men." It was a long shot, but maybe somebody was there with unusually large crystals that could be traced back to Virgil or something.

"Description? What is this? Cops and robbers?"

"Maybe." Kristy quickly explained what was going on, or rather what little she knew about what was going on.

"You get your little buns out of that house right now, Kristy Cunningham."

"I'm okay, Penny. I'm locked in with a very good watchdog." Who happened to be sprawled on the sofa snoring his head off at the moment.

"Okay—call you in the morning. Wait. Are there any hunks over there?"

As Mike's image floated across her mind's eye, she touched the tip of her nose. "Nah. Just some good old boys."

"That sounds suspicious, Kristy. Very suspicious."

"Oh, listen, has Mom called?"

"Yeah, and you owe me one, Kristy. I told her you'd taken off for parts unknown with someone named Wal-Mart or Hilton. She was beside herself. She was also on her way to some island with her garden club, so you're safe for now."

"Thanks, Penny."

At ten o'clock, Mercury was still snoring on the sofa and Kristy was propped up in the bed reading *Horoscopes, a Guide for Everyday Living* and trying to stay awake. She had on sweatpants, a silk pajama top, sneakers and her best underwear. Her mother would never forgive her if she got killed in ragged underwear, and her mother's reaction to her only daughter being bludgeoned without *any* underwear didn't bear thinking about.

Kristy was awakened, how much later she didn't know, by something. She lay still, hardly breathing, and listened. Katydids, a cricket chirping in the kitchen, Mercury snoring, nothing else. Then came a sound, ever so tiny, as if someone had bumped into one of the wire tables and the crystals had rattled against each other. She slipped out of bed and hefted the old rifle. Just as she got to the back door, the backyard exploded with sound. Dynamite was her first thought, and she threw herself off the porch and rolled, afraid the house might be hit next. Some bit of memory surfaced—probably from her cops and robbers movie phase—and she knew it hadn't been dynamite, but a shot. A shotgun.

When she heard something crashing through the woods—away from her—she raced into the house and snatched up the phone. She hated to turn on a light, but she couldn't see the stupid numbers. She compromised by turning on the desk lamp and throwing a chair cover over it. Mercury raised his head and yawned.

"Some great watchdog you are, Merc. Geez, we could be carried off and you'd never wake up." Her fingers shook as she tried to dial Mike's number. It rang. And rang. "If you don't answer this phone, Mike Ferguson, I will never speak to you again," she said as she counted the twelfth ring and slammed the phone down.

She turned the lamp off and scrunched up on the sofa beside the dog. She almost passed out from his aroma, but at least he was warm and breathing and she wasn't alone.

Within minutes, she heard footsteps on the porch, and a key turn in the lock. One part of her hoped it was Mike or Virgil; another part of her knew that everybody in Mount Ida, probably in the whole world, knew where Virgil kept his key.

She waited until the door eased open, then pointed the rifle and switched on the lamp. Mike stood there with his hand on the door knob. His shirt was unbuttoned almost to the waist, and as she watched, his expression seemed to melt from a fierce scowl to a look of relief. She could almost feel his taut muscles relax.

"That thing's not loaded. Don't you know it's dangerous to point an unloaded gun? It's an invitation for somebody to take it away from you."

She was in the mood for a little sympathy, a little "Are you okay," not a stupid gun lecture. "Where the blazes were you? You said to call— I called. Somebody's shooting at God only knows what with a shotgun, and you're not home."

"I'm here. It was probably hunters."

"Hunters? In the middle of the night? Well, that makes perfect sense to me."

"It's illegal. It's called spotting. They shine a light in a deer's face and—"

Her anxiety poured out in words. "Oh, give me a break, Mike. Not even poachers hunt deer with shotguns. So why aren't you out chasing the *hunters* instead of giving me your sportsman of the year lecture?"

"You okay?" He stood and watched her as if waiting for some reaction.

"Of course I'm okay. My trusty watchdog here scared them off. Either with his smell or his snoring. I'm not sure which."

"Hounds aren't into watching."

"I noticed. I suppose you were just in the neighborhood and decided to drop by?"

He leaned against the wall, arms crossed, and looked superior. "Actually I was . . . driving by and heard the gunshot. And I *did* check the woods, Kristy."

Suspicion bloomed. "Right. The old 'just driving by' routine."

"I think you need some coffee." He disappeared into the kitchen.

Kristy, now that she wasn't quite so frightened, decided she couldn't stand Mercury's smell a minute longer, and slipped off the sofa. When she wandered into the kitchen, Mike was standing with his back to her. His shirt was wet with sweat, even though the night was cool, and it stuck to him like a thin, blue, second skin. A leaf clung to his hair. She wanted more than anything to run to him, throw herself into those strong arms, have him tell her everything would be okay. But she wouldn't. She would hang tough. She wiped at the sweat trickling down her face and decided the night wasn't quite so cool as she had thought. Or she was having a delayed reaction to the excitement. Or...

"Well, have you had time to think up some cockamamy explanation for people running around shooting up the woods in the middle of the night? Other than deer poachers with shotguns?"

"I like the straight Giorgio scent better than Giorgio and dead rabbit." He turned and leaned back, his hands resting on the counter. The open wet shirt pulled apart slightly, exposing his chest. She could see the mat of golden hair curling down almost to his belt, where one button remained fastened. She wanted to reach out and touch his skin, see if it was as silky as she thought it might be. She quickly looked up... into his eyes.

His gaze met hers, then moved on until he had examined her thoroughly. "Aren't you burning up in all those clothes?"

"I'm just fine in all these clothes." She refused to touch the droplet of sweat about to slip from her nose.

"I suppose you went to sleep in them. Just in case the bad guys came back?"

"Don't be absurd. I was working on my astrological chart for the coming year. No one would sleep in this many clothes."

He reached out and touched the collar of her pajama top. "Unless they were afraid and wouldn't admit it. But I don't know. Silk and sweatpants?"

She needed to brush his hand away but couldn't seem to manage it. "They were handy."

"Ummm." He turned to the stove and poured two mugs of coffee. When she took hers, he put his arm around her and led her into the living room. She wanted to wiggle out of his grasp...except she might spill the hot coffee...and he might spill his hot coffee and...

"Out, Merc," Mike said. "Go chase a bunny." The dog stretched and yawned, but finally got off the sofa and went out the door. Kristy sat in the rocking chair, and Mike settled into an overstuffed chair and stared at her. "You must be tougher than I thought."

"Why? Because I'm not a basket case?" She was, inside, but she was not about to let him know that.

"I thought maybe—"

"Well, you thought wrong." She had every intention of falling apart, but not until he left. "You can go home. I don't think they'll be back."

He sipped the hot coffee. "But one never knows, does one? I think I'd better stay for a while."

"A while?" Her skin prickled all over from the heat.

"Maybe all night."

"All night?"

"What's the matter, Kristy? Did something happen to your hearing?"

"Hea—? No. I'm fine. You can't stay here all night."

He shrugged. "Well, you won't go home with me. And you won't go to a motel. So, I'll just stay here."

"Oh." Kristy couldn't think of another thing to say to him. The silence lay between them like an impenetrable fog.

"Why didn't you ever come back?" he asked at last.

"Back where?"

"Here, Kristy. To see Virgil."

She heard something in his voice that made her sit up a little straighter. Not an edge, more of a...wistfulness. No...it sounded the way she had felt after her parents' divorce, when she realized her father wasn't going to come home every evening from work, wasn't ever coming home again. It was a mixture of hurt and anger and, yes, wistfulness, a plea for someone to explain, to make it all right again. It suddenly became very important that she make him understand why she had never come back. Except it was very hard to explain something you didn't completely understand yourself. It all had to do with dreams and illusions and memories so vivid and fine and a part of her that she was afraid to tamper with.

She wanted to tell him all this, but somehow she didn't think Mike Ferguson was a man who dealt in dreams and memories. She finally shrugged. "I don't think you'd understand."

"Try me."

She twisted a strand of hair around her finger. "I was afraid, I guess. That it wouldn't be the same."

"It's never the same, Kristy, but that's not good enough. Lord, you're all he ever talked about. I probably know as much about your exploits in college as you do."

Kristy shifted uncomfortably. "Real impressive track record, huh?" When he didn't respond, she tried again. "Granddad's letters were what kept me going during that awful period after Mom and Dad's divorce. I felt like Daddy had abandoned me, but Granddad was always there. I meant to come back. Mom and I had terrible fights about it. I even ran away once and tried to hitchhike here. Then I started college, and Mom couldn't stop me from visiting, but by then it seemed too late. I...I just didn't come. I had relived those summers for so long, I was afraid I would get here and there would be nothing but a bunch of rocks and an old man. And no magic. I wanted to keep the magic of this place forever, Mike. I didn't know it would still be here."

He stood up and paced the floor for a moment, then sat on the footstool in front of her. "You can't just wander into someone's life every ten years or so and wander back out without leaving hurt behind."

"I wouldn't hurt Granddad for anything."

"I know your intentions are good, Kristy, but in the end, you will leave. Just like Garrett did. God, Kristy, you don't know what Virgil was like when he found out your dad had sneaked off in the night. He went crazy. He started drinking, got mean. Chester was the only one who hung tough with him. When I was just a little kid, I remember going with Chester late at night to drag Virgil out of some bar where somebody was getting ready to stomp his head."

Kristy tried not to let the shock she felt show on her face. "I didn't know Granddad ever drank."

Mike's laugh was bitter. "He tried to drink this whole part of the world dry. He quit when you were born. Just quit the day he got the announcement. Worked his butt off for five years before he would ask if you could come see him. Chester called Garrett and told him Virgil had been sober all those years."

Kristy fought back the tears. "Lord, Mike, I didn't know any of this. But it won't happen like that again. Surely you know that."

"I wish I did." He got up and paced. "You'll get him used to having you here, make him think you're going to stay forever, then you'll leave and won't come back."

"I *will* come back," she said.

"No, Kristy. It's the excitement you want, the something new. Virgil doesn't need excitement at his age. He also doesn't need anyone on a white horse riding in when she feels like it."

Kristy looked away from his fierce look. "What makes you an authority on what Granddad needs?"

He pointed a finger at her. "I owe Virgil a lot, including a little peace and quiet in his old age, and I won't let him go through that hell again."

She snapped a look at him. "I am not my father, Mike, and what is between fathers and sons is different from any other relationship in the world. And if I leave, it will be in the light of day, not in the middle of the night. Didn't it ever occur to you that Daddy may have had his reasons? He might have thought it would be easier for both of them?"

"Well, it wasn't, was it? I love that old man, Kristy, and I won't let you hurt him with your games."

"Games! I'm here because I love that old man, too."

"Well you sure as hell have a funny way of showing it." His eyes blazed with emotion.

When he sat down on the footstool again, she picked at a loose thread on the chair arm. "Besides, I may not go home. I may just stay here."

"Right. There's a lot to interest a jet-setter like you in Mount Ida."

"I am not a jet-setter." She sought his eyes. "And there are a lot of things here that interest me." Not the least of which was this man sitting in front of her. She desperately searched for some way to tell him who she was, what she wanted to do with her life, but she knew he wouldn't believe her. Wouldn't believe she could be content right here, working with the beautiful crystals.

Something changed in his expression. He reached up and trailed a finger down the front of her pajama top. "I believe that *you* believe that, Kristy, but I don't. You'd get bored with a place like this."

"How can you get bored, when every day's like Christmas?" she asked softly, willing him to understand, to give her a chance.

"The Christmas part is the small part. The big part is hard, dirty work. That's what Garrett finally couldn't deal with." He smoothed the hair away from her face, his fingers lingering on her cheek.

"You still want me to leave." She could hardly breathe.

"You need to go back to your life, Kristy, let us get back to ours."

She felt his heat, sensed his desire and could not be sure whether he was speaking of what was good for her grandfather—or what was good for him. His hand moved from her cheek and cupped the back of her neck, gently pulling her toward him. She felt the warmth of his body mingle with a sudden heat of her own. When his lips touched hers, she reached up and touched his face. He pulled her to him in a fierce hug, and his hands explored her back while his lips demanded more of her.

When at last he pulled away, need flickered in his eyes, and he shuddered with an effort to control himself. "Don't you know how easy it is for a man to love a beautiful young woman? Come to depend on her being there? What it would do to his heart when she left?'' When his lips touched hers again, they were gentle and tasted of a bittersweet goodbye.

The bittersweet kiss told her he was not talking about his own heart. He quickly stood up. ''It would be better for everyone.''

She stood and faced him, struggling to control her rampant feelings and emotions, afraid this was her last chance to make him understand. ''Do you really think Granddad's so fragile that he can't deal with my leaving? If you do, you give darn little credit to that old man.''

''No. What I think is that you will make promises you can't keep. I think I was wrong to think I should stay the night. You'll be just fine now. I'm going home,'' he said in a tense voice. ''And Kristy, jet-setters do not sleep in underwear and sweatpants.''

She followed him to the door. ''What would you know about their underwear and, and— You don't know anything about me, Mike. And if you cared that much about Granddad, you wouldn't have lost him.''

After Mike left she sat on the porch until her body temperature felt normal again. She lectured Mercury on all the reasons she could not possibly even like, let alone love, a man like Mike. But in the end, she knew she was already in love with him. And when she did leave, she would be the one hurt, not Virgil, and obviously not Mike.

She pushed the thoughts of him out of her mind— mostly—and concentrated on the problem of Virgil. And the mine. And whoever had ransacked the house. Just as the sun fired the eastern sky with reds and pinks, she called her father. She had an idea. Perhaps if she could find the lost crystals, Virgil would come back and Mike would settle down and . . . and what? Her father took a long time to answer the phone.

"Did I wake you up, Daddy?"

"No, baby, I always get up before daylight."

"Daddy, it's daylight here, so it has to be daylight in Atlanta."

"Fine, great, so it's daylight. That's the thing I always hated most about the rural life. People get up at the most god-awful hours. How are you?"

"I'm fine, Daddy. Did Granddad ever tell you about any crystals he buried during the war?" She heard him stifle a yawn.

"Crystals during the war?"

"Wake up. This is important."

"He mined during the war."

"I know that, Daddy, but did he ever tell you that he buried some really big pieces? For later."

"Hmmm. I don't think so. He was always rambling about how my future was taken care of, how there'd be enough to set me up in mining, everything. But that was before he realized that I didn't want to spend my life with the rocks."

"That's it!" Excitement flooded through Kristy. "Now think carefully, Daddy. Did he ever tell you about any special place? Take you somewhere when he told you about your future being secure and such?"

"Honey, that was all a long time ago."

"Please, it's important." She heard him yawn again.

"Uh, I don't know." There was a long silence. "There was a place we used to go sometimes, not too far from the house. We owned the land at one time, but Virgil got into one of his usual financial binds and sold it. A paper company I think, or maybe the national forest.''

"Where? Where was it?"

"I have no idea. But there was a wet weather creek...and I remember a huge pine tree that had a burn scar on it. Virgil always said that old pine would be there when we were all dead and gone."

"You're a peach, Daddy. Go back to bed."

"Kristy, what is going on?"

"Tell you later. Bye. Daddy, wait. Did you ever think about coming back for a visit?"

There was a long silence. "Yeah, baby, I've thought about it. I don't think I'd be too welcome."

"I'll work on it. Bye." She could almost see her poor father sitting on the side of the bed, staring at the phone and scratching his head. But she remembered Virgil taking her to the same place her father had described. Except the last time they'd gone, there'd only been a huge stump, which had annoyed Virgil greatly. A stump and some funny rock formation.

She called Mercury and started out through the woods, certain she could go right to the place. As she walked, she wondered why Mike wouldn't admit the existence of the lost crystals. Well, she would show him. She would find them. And maybe she would find her grandfather.

By noon, she had tramped for miles in every direction from the house and found absolutely nothing that looked the least bit familiar. As she walked up the back steps, the phone rang.

CHAPTER TEN

WHEN KRISTY snatched up the receiver, she was relieved to hear Penny's voice. "Kristy, there were scads of people from Arkansas," Penny said with an air of irritation.

"Like who?"

"Like a young woman, mid-thirties, blond hair, blue eyes with crystals hanging from her ears and nose, name Sun and Air. Geez, Kristy, there are some strange people in this thing. I've been thinking that maybe, instead of industrial, we ought to go New Age. They seem to have all the money. Now if we set up—"

"Penny! Who else?" She listened patiently as her friend went through a long list of very detailed descriptions, none of which sounded like anyone she knew. She had almost dozed off when something Penny said rang a bell in her brain. "Wait, run that one by again."

"Man, early forties, real serious, works out in the sun, khaki shirt."

Kristy ran through her list of suspects. "Was he going bald?"

"How would I know? He had a cap on."

"Well, how many people wear caps inside a building?"

"Lord, I don't know. Probably a bunch. This is Texas. Am I supposed to go back and ask him to take his cap off?"

"No, it has to be John Graves, a forestry service guy." Unless, of course, it was someone she didn't even know. What would John Graves be doing at a crystal show in Dallas?

"Come to think of it, it looked like there had been some kind of patch or insignia on his shirt once. You know how the material kind of puckers and looks different when you take one off?"

"Forestry Service patch. What was he selling?"

"Some really big stuff. Nice. I tried to talk to him about marketing, but he just smiled and looked serious."

"You're a jewel, Penny. Thanks."

"But Kristy, what about a corporation?"

"Later. I'll explain it all later." Although her eyes were scratchy from lack of sleep, her growing excitement pushed the exhaustion aside. It was possible, it even made sense. John Graves was in a perfect position to direct a gang of poachers. After all, he knew where all the good digs were, knew exactly what was coming out of the ground. And he would certainly know all the oldtimers and their stories. And he had two very convenient scapegoats that he could never seem to catch.

She ran out to the car and headed for the mine, Mercury panting in the front seat beside her. She could just see Mike's look of surprise when she told him. Then the look of surprise would change to one of awe and pride, and he would take her in his arms...and she almost ran the car off the road.

When she got to the mine, Mike was not there. She had started to leave when he came tearing up the road in his truck, almost lost in a cloud of dust. From the look in his eyes when he stepped out of the truck, she knew he was as mad as a wet hen. Kristy swallowed hard and walked toward him.

"I know who's behind all the dynamiting and the house and everything," she told him in a rush.

"Really?"

"John Graves." She went on to explain about the crystal show and Penny and her theory. "So, you probably need to get Granddad. Graves is supposed to be looking for him, but obviously for all the wrong reasons. Or worse still, he may have found Granddad."

Mike shook his head. "You don't have the slightest idea what you're talking about, Kristy, and I don't have time to listen to your cops and robbers theories."

"But he had that big crystal. And he told me he didn't know how much to charge for Virgil's crystals. And I talked to Daddy and I know where they are... more or less."

Mike sighed. "Kristy, you are creating mysteries where there are no mysteries. Everyone around here, including John Graves, digs a few rocks."

"But how do you explain—"

"There is nothing to explain. I've known John Graves most of my life. He's solid as a rock."

"One of the good old boys, huh? Well, that certainly takes care of that. Good old boys don't do bad things. Only outsiders do bad things. Right?"

"Wrong. Now if you will excuse me, I have things to do." He opened the truck's passenger door. "Come on, Merc, you can keep me company today." The dog sailed out of Kristy's convertible and into the pickup.

"Traitor," Kristy called after them. "One lousy bath and you turn on me, Merc."

As Kristy drove home, the lack of sleep finally caught up with her. She felt bone tired. Before she went to bed for the day, she called Mr. Eldridge. She might as well try her theory out on him. She quickly explained everything she knew or suspected.

"Oh dear, Miss Kristy," Sam said, "John's a local boy. I don't think he'd do anything like that."

She thought she detected a trace of uncertainty in his voice, and his denial of the possibility was not that vigorous. "How do you know that?"

"Well, I don't *know* anything, but John takes his work quite seriously, and he has a lovely family. Of course, they do have some new rangers and such, and there are always Job Corps boys, some of whom come from very questionable backgrounds in my opinion, but... the sheriff assures me he is combing the woods for Virgil."

The sheriff no doubt assured Mr. Eldridge of whatever he wanted to be assured of. "Well, it was just a thought."

"Of course, and a very disturbing one, I might add."

Kristy said her goodbyes and tried not to slam the phone down. How very disturbing to everyone that an outsider would even suggest that one of the locals might be involved. She might be Virgil Cunningham's granddaughter, but she was still an outsider, and she guessed she always would be. Right now she was too worn out to even get mad about it. She went into the bedroom and crashed.

She was awakened sometime in the afternoon by a knock on the door. She struggled out of a deep sleep and stumbled down the hall.

"Miss Cunningham?"

Kristy realized with a sinking feeling that the voice coming from the shadows of the front porch belonged to John Graves. She supposed he'd come to kill her or something, but she was too tired to care. "Yes?"

"We caught those two boys early this morning. West of here with a load of stolen crystals. I think they're the ones who've been poaching on your grandpa's land."

"Oh?" She carefully kept the screen door between them.

"They're local boys, from over around Jessieville. Said they were working alone. I'm hoping the sheriff can scare the truth out of them."

"Great. Thanks for coming by."

"Miss Cunningham, I think maybe they know something about Virgil."

Kristy tensed and took a deep breath. "Like what?"

"I don't know. But our men have been keeping an eye out, and we haven't found a trace of Virgil. It doesn't look good. Mike asked me to throw the Job Corps boys into the search."

"Mike?" Mike was asking for a search? She shivered in the afternoon heat. "Thanks." She turned away from the door, leaving him standing on the porch.

Kristy lay on the bed, her mind in a turmoil. If Mike had launched an all-out search for Virgil, then things were terribly amiss. She didn't want to believe John Graves—she wanted him to be the bad guy—because if she believed him, then she had to admit that something had happened to Virgil, had to admit that Mike was thinking along the same lines suddenly. And that just would not do. That would not do at all. As she tried to convince herself that John Graves was merely trying to scare her, that he was involved somehow, that Mike was really out in the woods drinking boiled coffee with Virgil and talking about the mine, the tears came, and after the tears, she fell into a restless sleep of exhaustion.

When she opened her eyes, the house was dark. She listened for whatever it was that had awakened her, and after a long moment heard it again. Someone rustling papers on the desk. She slipped out of bed, picked up the rifle and tiptoed down the hall.

She aimed the gun and flipped on the light. When the old man looked up from the desk, his whiskered face broke into a smile.

"That thing ain't loaded, honey. I don't know when I ever had any shells for it."

"Granddad!" She dropped the gun and threw herself at him.

He held her for a moment, patting her awkwardly, then held her at arm's length. "You'll get all dirty huggin' me, honey. I like to had a heart attack, walkin' in here and findin' you in bed all curled up just like you was a little girl again. Lord, ain't you a sight for sore eyes. All growed up and purty as a picture. I'm gonna get me a handful of that boy, keepin' you here all to himself, not sayin' a word."

Kristy smiled and wiped the tears away.

"Here, now, what are you cryin' about, honey? Am I that awful lookin'?"

"You look wonderful. I was afraid something awful had happened to you, Granddad."

"I'm too ornery to kill, honey, but it has been an excitin' week. You seen Mikey? I been lookin' for that boy all day." He picked up the phone.

As Kristy wiped her tears, Virgil's words began to sink in. "Not sayin' a word," and "like to had a heart attack, findin' you . . ." Realization slowly seeped into her mind, and everything began to come together. She had come to accept the fact that Mike knew where Virgil was and didn't trust her enough to tell her. She had come to believe that he just hadn't bothered to go find Virgil. After all, if he didn't see Virgil, he didn't have to tell him his granddaughter was here. But Mike had *seen* Virgil, had *talked* to him in the past few days. And he hadn't told Virgil she was here. He had found him, he had... try as she might, she could find no way to reconcile that. She felt an ache begin deep inside her, an ache unlike any she had ever known. Virgil hung up the phone and smiled at her.

"You are a sight, Kristy, honey. When'd you get in?"

"Last Sunday night. Mike didn't tell you?" she asked in a shaky voice.

"Honey, you think I'd of stayed out there if I'd known my baby was here? He better have a good reason. I thought there was somebody in the house last night, but I figured it was Mikey."

"I'll make some coffee." She hurried to the kitchen to pull herself together and get her thoughts organized. She wanted to talk to Virgil without Mike around, she wanted some explanation of Mike's behavior, wanted her grandfather to tell her that it had all been some scheme of his, not Mike's. But even now she knew better. "I want to know everything that happened, Granddad," she called.

"It's a long story, honey."

She put the coffee on to heat and came to sit on the floor at Virgil's feet, just as she had done all those years ago. "So I have a long time to listen."

"Wellsir, I found me a pocket of rocks durin' the war. Oh, honey, wait till you see 'em. Me and Chester."

"Arvin told me a little bit. Mike said it was a legend."

"Dern Arvin, he musta told half the county. Anyhow, there's been some real strange folks around here all summer. Come in from somewhere out west. Hired a gang from over north of Jessieville to dig for 'em.''

He was interrupted by the sound of a truck. Before he could continue, Mercury flew through the door and landed right in the middle of Virgil, whining and howling and licking the old man's face.

"You old potlicker, get offa me. You're gonna smother me," Virgil yelled. "I saw you just yesterday."

Mike stood in the doorway. "Dammit, Virgil, that dog and I have been all over these woods today looking for you. Where were you?"

"Followin' a couple of boys around, that's where. Boys that been a mite too interested in my business."

Mike's voice was stern, but Kristy heard the softness underneath, the deep, abiding love for Virgil. "You weren't supposed to do that. You were supposed to call me."

"Didn't have time, boy."

Kristy excused herself to get the coffee. Not, she thought, that anyone would even notice she was gone. They were in their own world now, a world she was not a part of. It had all been their little secret, their little game. She poured coffee with a shaky hand and took the cups to the men.

Virgil took a swallow of the brew. "Oh, that's mighty fine, honey. Better than that boiled stuff I been drinkin'. Mikey, you shoulda seen those boys scat outta here last night after I drew down with that old shotgun. Like turpentined cats."

Kristy coughed loudly. "Would anyone like to tell me what's going on?"

Virgil laughed. "Oh, honey, it was a sight. Anyhow, like I was tellin' you. Chester and me buried these rocks and spent twenty years tryin' to forget they were there."

"Oh, yes, the rocks that don't exist." She glared at Mike. "Why on earth would you try to forget them?" she asked.

"Well. There was some hard times. I knew I'd be tempted to dig 'em up and sell 'em. Like Chester did, God rest his soul. Course Chester dug his up right after Mikey was born and put it all into a good mine. Wanted the boy to have a start in the business. I was savin' mine. First for your daddy, then for you. Wellsir, in all them years, I never forgot they was there, but I dern sure forgot where they was." He laughed. "Damn paper companies kept buyin' and cuttin' and replantin' and by the time I got to lookin' again, nothin' looked the same." He grinned sheepishly. "Me and Chester drank a bit back in those days, and I guess maybe I didn't pay as much attention to my buryin' place as Chester did his."

Kristy shot Mike a look intended to kill. "And the new mine? The one Mike has allegedly put so much of his hard earned money into?"

Virgil slapped his knee and laughed. "Why there ain't enough rocks in that ground to support a widow woman." He leaned close to Kristy. "That's what ever'body thinks, anyway. But I've had my eye on that old mine for twenty years. I got a feelin' about it. I think we're within two weeks of hittin' paydirt. I was gonna write you about it, but I wanted to wait till we hit it big. Anyhow, Mikey and me got wind that this outfit from out west was lookin' for all those old caches the oldtimers talk about."

"Santa Fe, Granddad. I think maybe I sold some of your crystals to one of their spies."

"Could be, honey. Anyhow, things started gettin' a little rough around here. So we put all our time—and a bit of Mikey's money—into buyin' that old mine so ever'body'd think that's where the big stuff was." He waggled a finger at Kristy. "And you just wait and see. I'm right about that old mine."

Kristy smiled at her grandfather, willing to go along with his dreams, just as Mike had.

Mike smiled at her. "The ruse worked for a while. Except someone didn't buy it. They came to see Virgil, took him out in the woods and tried to persuade him to talk. He got away and rolled down a bluff. The fall would have killed anyone else." He squeezed the old man's arm. "We decided he ought to play dead for a while. Or at least stay missing, so whoever was behind the attack would think he was dead. Maybe bring someone out in the open."

Kristy listened, getting madder at the two men by the moment. "So, *have* you two found out who did it?"

Mike spoke. "John Graves caught two men today. Probably the ones Virgil was following. They say they're working for some guru in Santa Fe. Virgil can go take a look at them first thing in the morning and see if they're the ones."

"Oh, they're the ones, all right," Virgil said, nodding vigorously. He pointed to Kristy. "I guess you showin' up threw a real monkey wrench in the gears."

"So I've been told," she said calmly. Kristy wanted the rest of the story before she blew a gasket. "And the dynamiting?"

Virgil laughed. "That was me, lookin' for them dern rocks."

She stood up and stared at Mike. "And, of course, you were going out to check on him every day or two. And Mercury was running off to spend the nights with him." Even the stupid dog was a traitor.

"What'd you wash Mercury with, honey? I near 'bout couldn't stand him for two days."

Mike met her eyes. "I have to admit that when you found that damn note, Kristy, I was worried. I *thought* it was an old one, but I couldn't be sure."

"You were worried? Good. You had all of what? A few hours to worry? Well I've been worried sick for a week. You could have told me everything." She pointed a finger at Mike. "And you could have told Granddad I was here."

She saw the realization of what he had done dawn on him, but it was too late as far as she was concerned. "Kristy, that's why I went looking for him today. I . . . after last night, I knew—"

"Oh, right, Mike," she said. "Well it's too late for explanations. You're both acting like a couple of kids."

The two men stared at her in silence. Virgil was the first to break it. "Kristy, honey, he probably did right. He knew I'd come flyin' back here to see you. And the ones wanting my rocks might have come after you if they thought you knew anything. Mikey was just thinkin' about you, honey."

"They came after me, anyway," she answered, but it was to Mike, not her grandfather. She didn't believe for one minute that any danger to her had one thing to do with why Mike hadn't told Virgil she was here. It was Mike trying to protect Virgil from his granddaughter. "But everyone knows girls can't keep secrets. And they certainly spill their guts if anyone threatens them. Right, Mike?"

Mike frowned. "Kristy, after we talked, I...dammit, I was trying to protect you. These people play hard-ball."

"You didn't trust me," she snapped. "And I don't *need* protecting."

Virgil leaned forward in his chair and shook his head, obviously upset. "Kristy, honey—"

Mike put his hands on her shoulders. "You do need protecting. We knew that whoever came nosing around here were the rock hunters we were looking for. And I was keeping an eye on you most of the time. But they might have come when I wasn't around. It wasn't safe for you to know too much."

She started to respond, then didn't. What was the use? They both saw her as the outsider, as the little girl they'd known years ago. It was all right for her grand-father to see her that way, but she couldn't bear to have Mike see her that way. "Never mind." She stood up and started out of the room.

Mike grabbed her arm and pulled her close. "Do you want to hear my side of it or not?"

She pulled away. "No, Mike. I don't think you have a side. Now if you will excuse me, I'm going to bed."

He stayed her with a hand. "Kristy," he said softly, "It's not the way you think it was."

"Right. Granddad, you need to call Mr. Eldridge. He's been worried sick." She went to the bedroom and shut the door. She could hear their voices, but they were low, and she couldn't make out anything they said. She put on her silk pajamas, this time without the under-wear, brushed her hair, splashed Giorgio perfume on liberally and marched back into the living room. The two men looked up from their table-full of papers. Mercury sniffed her and set up a mournful howl.

She put a hand against the wall and gave them a Joan Crawford poise. "If you *gentlemen* can spare me a moment." She smiled through clenched teeth. "I know where your darn rocks are." With that she marched back to the bedroom, slammed the door and ignored their entreaties to come out and tell them more.

At least she'd got their attention. And she did know—more or less—where their darn rocks were.

CHAPTER ELEVEN

THE HOUSE was empty when Kristy got up. She sat on the back porch and drank coffee and knew it was time to think about going home. She had spent half the night trying to convince herself that Mike *had* been trying to protect her, that what he had tried to tell her when she cut him off had been a rational, logical explanation. That their excluding her from their reunion last night had been just heat-of-the-moment stuff, a result of Mike's relief that Virgil was safe after a long day of looking for him, and Virgil's excitement over the chase. She'd spent the other half of the night trying to convince herself that she could fit into their lives.

All of which had come to little except a sleepless night, because everything still came down to trust and love and all those things for which explanations should be unnecessary.

She was still sitting there when she heard the truck and saw the two men walk around the side of the house.

"Kristy, honey, we been down to the jail. They got them boys. They were workin' for some crazy guru in Santa Fe, sure as hell. And that woman you was talkin' about? I guess she was part of it, but she's taken off. Damn furriners comin' in here messin' with us. Well-sir, they'll find out what it's like to spend a long vacation in the cotton fields."

She didn't point out that the only ones who were likely to go to prison were the local boys who had gotten caught. But the crisis was over, with everything neatly solved, which she supposed was her cue to go home. Except she didn't want to go home. "I'm glad, Granddad. I guess everything's wrapped up now."

"Not just yet, honey. You and me and Mikey are gonna go find them buried rocks today. Now you just tell me what it is you figured out."

Kristy could have kissed her grandfather. It was as if he had given her a reprieve. She looked at Mike, but he was busy scratching Mercury's ears. He hadn't spoken a word to her since last night. "Well, I don't know *exactly* where they are, but..." She related the conversation she'd had with her father and the things she remembered.

Virgil was quiet for a long moment. "I'll swear. So your daddy does remember a few things about this place. I thought he'd forgot all of it." He shook his head. "Well, what are we waitin' for? Can't be too many places like that close by. It's the damn burned pine I been lookin' for all this time. Many times as me and Chester took you there and I up and forgot all about it bein' cut down. You'd sit on a rock and eat your dinner. No wonder I couldn't find it."

Virgil led them to a place beside the creek that he thought fit the description. The creek bank was badly eroded, and the hillside leading up from it had been clear-cut and replanted perhaps ten years ago. There was no burned pine tree, nor was there any stump that might have been the pine.

Mike paced the creek bank. "The stump could have washed away, Virgil. This creek gets high and wide every couple of years in the spring."

"Might have. But the place don't feel just right. The older I get, the more this country all looks alike. Honey? How 'bout it?"

She shook her head. "I don't recognize anything." Something gnawed at her, just below the edge of consciousness. There had been something different about the place she recalled. Something that had fired her child's imagination, filled her with delight when Virgil took her there.

They walked along the creek for perhaps a mile. Mike was distant, seemingly wrapped up in his own thoughts. He had tried to talk to her when they left the house, but she had shut him out and hurried along to talk to her grandfather, afraid Mike would give her explanations that wouldn't ring true, tell her all the reasons he had been right, instead of saying the simple words admitting he had been wrong. And his words would sound right and logical and smooth, and they would break her heart.

When they came to a wide place with a rock ledge, they stopped. Mike looked at Virgil. "Why don't you two rest a bit and I'll check out this section. See if anything looks like what you described."

Virgil sat down and wiped his face with a bandanna. "Fool paper companies."

Kristy sat down, glad of the rest.

"Your daddy doin' all right, honey?"

Kristy heard the strain in his voice. "Fine." She picked up a pine needle and twisted it around her finger. "Granddad, what happened between you and Daddy?"

Virgil shook his head. "Stubbornness, I reckon. Both of us."

She waited and studied her grandfather. He was an old man now, and while he appeared to be in good health, how many years did he have left?

"Oh, I was proud of that boy. Smart as a whip. But stubborn. His momma knew just how to handle him, but I was always quite a hand to try to bull my way through things I ought to have tiptoed through. After she died, wasn't nobody to keep us on the straight and narrow."

"I think he'd like to see you." The words came out without her thinking. Her father had certainly never mentioned the desire to see his father, but too many years had passed in anger. Kristy wanted more than anything in the world for them to get back together. Before it was too late.

"I doubt that, honey. Not that I blame him a bit. I was awful hard on the boy when he told me he wanted to go off to college instead of work rocks with me. I reckon I'd had my heart set on us workin' together for so long, why, I just couldn't think about anything else." Virgil twisted and untwisted his bandanna. "I thought it was a phase, thought he'd still come back. And he did. He worked every summer—except that last one. Oh, he came back that summer, but just to tell me he wouldn't be stayin'. He'd met your momma. I guess I threw a right smart fit, sent him to his room like you would a kid." Virgil's eyes glistened in the morning sun. "Next mornin' he was gone. Your momma still a hard woman?"

Kristy laughed. "Still hard as nails where the Cunningham men are concerned."

"Whooee, that woman and me struck fire soon as we met. I visited 'em once in Texas, back when Garrett was still tryin' to make things right. I wasn't in the mood yet, I guess, and your momma and me struck fire right off. Why, she told me when to wash, what to wear, gave me to understand right quick, tho' she never put it in words, wasn't no hick in-laws gonna embarrass her.''

"That's Mom. She's mellowed a little, though.''

"She needed to mellow out more than a little, honey.'' His voice trailed away. "She made a man feel like he wasn't worth nothin' to nobody if he didn't wear a suit and talk just right. I thought your daddy gettin' away from her was one of the smarter things he did.''

"She wanted him to be something he wasn't. I mean he's a big banker and all that, but he's still got a lot of these mountains in him, Granddad. He wanted to work in his garden on Saturdays, Mom wanted to hang around the club. With the important people.'' Her mind began to work on the logistics of getting her father home for a visit. "You and Daddy could be friends.''

"Hard words are hard to take back, honey. Mighty hard. The closest we come was after I quit drinkin' and asked could my little granddaughter come see me. I've started many a letter to him, but I never sent 'em.''

Kristy looked up in surprise. "Why not?''

"Old man's pride, honey. Old man's pride. Afraid he wouldn't answer 'em.''

"Oh, Granddad, he would have.'' She wondered if her father had done the same thing over the years.

"Maybe. But what if he hadn't?''

"So you just adopted Mike, right?''

Virgil chuckled, "I reckon you might say that. Tried to do right by him. His daddy run off when he was little, and Mikey started gettin' in with a bad crowd. Wouldn't listen to Chester, so Chester brought him to me. Oh, that boy was a mess when I put him to work. Chip on his shoulder big enough to drive a truck on.

Course I was a mess myself. I'd give up the drink, but I hadn't give up my mad.''

Kristy thought Mike still had a chip on his shoulder, but didn't bother to point it out.

"Headed right for jail, he was.''

"Jail? Mr. Perfect in jail?'' She couldn't believe what she was hearing.

"I worked him till he liked to drop. And I stayed with him till I liked to drop. We had us some go-rounds. But after a bit, he fell right into rock diggin' like he'd been born in a mine. I reckon I got rid of my hurtin' over Garrett through that boy. After that summer, I asked could you come. I reckon you musta been about six or seven when you first come here.''

"Mike was all the things daddy never was, right?''

"I reckon so. You really think your daddy and me might could get together?''

"Yeah, I sure do.'' She would arrange it, if she had to hogtie both of them and drag them together.

She stood up when she heard Mike approaching. She could tell by the expression on his face that he hadn't found anything.

As if reading her mind, he glared at her. "I thought you knew where they were.''

"I never said I knew exactly. I said I thought I knew. I didn't say I could walk right to them.''

"Right.''

"Well, you're the one who's supposed to know every inch of this country. Surely you can find one lousy tree stump, beside a creek, with rocks.''

"Rocks?''

She frowned. "Rocks. There were some kind of funny rocks.''

"Funny rocks," he said sarcastically. "Well, that surely does pin it right down to one of a million places."

Virgil waved his bandana in their direction. "Lord a mercy, you two sound just like you did years ago. I never in my life saw two youngins fight like you two did." He stood up. "No use arguin' about it. There *was* some big rocks."

Mike shook his head. "Which were probably hauled off to landscape some subdivision over on the lake twenty years ago."

Virgil stood up and pocketed his bandanna. "Look, we might as well go to the house and think on this some more. Maybe Kristy'll remember about them rocks. I never was much of one to notice rocks. It was trees I marked by. Lot of good that did me."

They trudged back to the house, all of them tired and out of sorts.

Mike gave Kristy a tight smile. "If you have any sort of seizure or vision, let me know. Meanwhile, I have a couple of mines to run."

Before she could snap at him, Virgil put his arm around her. "Now you go easy on my baby, boy. Not her fault she can't pull the rabbit out of the hat right off. She just needs a little time to think on it."

"Right." Mike drove out of the driveway as if he were on a racetrack.

"He may be a good substitute for a son, Granddad, but I cannot tell you how much I despise that man."

Virgil slapped his leg and whooped with laughter. "Oh, I can see that, Kristy, honey. I surely can see that."

"What's so funny?"

"Shoot, honey, that boy's so struck on you he don't know whether he's comin' or goin'. And you stare at him like a moonsick calf."

Kristy looked at her grandfather as if he had taken total leave of his senses. She started to tell him all the reasons he was wrong, when really she wanted to tell him how she felt about Mike, tell him all the things she would have put in a letter to him. But the truth was too hard to face. "That's ridiculous. He's a Virgo," she said, as if to shrug the whole thing off.

"No, honey, he's a Ferguson, and them Fergusons always get what they go after. I believe I'll just take me a nap, honey."

Kristy stood in the yard and stared at nothing. Virgil was just doing a lot of wishful thinking. His surrogate son and his beloved granddaughter living happily ever after— If he only had any idea how much she wished it were true.

WHEN KRISTY got up the next morning, Virgil was busy in the backyard, cleaning and cooking crystals. Mercury lay sprawled in a hole he had dug, looking very pleased with himself and the world. His eyes tracked Virgil's every movement like a fine-tuned radar. She smiled at the scene and began unwrapping the crystals that were left in the baskets.

"Look at this one, honey." Virgil held a point, not a particularly good one, close to her. "Now see here at the base where it broke off the plate?" She nodded. "See how smooth it is? And see this little point right inside that smooth part? Little thing started to heal itself."

"Heal itself?"

"Why, sure. Broke off and in time, that break'd heal and start growin' again in the earth. Prob'ly broke off before them dinosaurs was even thought of."

Kristy examined the point in awed silence. "You mean it's growing right now?"

"No, honey. It did what it could millions of years ago. Ain't nobody ever seen this but you and me, honey," he said quietly.

Before the day was over, Virgil had given her a wealth of information about crystals and speculated at great length at the cataclysmic forces and hot water that had formed them. The more he talked, the more awestruck Kristy felt, the more humbled by this force of nature that had created such beauty and perfection. He talked about special crystals he had found, veins and pockets. He talked about every day being like Christmas. And Kristy began to understand, really understand for the first time, that in spite of Virgil's great dreams of "the big one," none of the digging had anything to do with money. The "big one" was a bigger crystal, a more perfect one, a point clearer than all other points. It had to do with finding them and seeing them for the first time. Mike had tried to tell her, but she hadn't understood . . . until now.

And by afternoon, she had begun to burn with some of Virgil's fever, which was stronger than Arvin's fever, stronger even than Mike's. She burned with a desire to go into the mountains and find a pocket of crystals that would be more beautiful and more spectacular than any pocket ever opened.

They had loaded the tanks when Mr. Eldridge walked around the house. He nodded to Kristy but went directly to Virgil and slapped him on the back. "Virgil, you rascal, I trust you are quite pleased with yourself, worrying us all into a state of apoplexy.''

Virgil grinned. ''Dern it, Sam, callin' my baby and scarin' her half to death. You ought to be ashamed.'' He looked sheepishly at Kristy. ''I'm sure glad you did, though. Ain't she a sight?''

The lawyer smiled at Kristy. ''She surely is. And showing definite signs of becoming a fine business-woman, I might add. Why she stepped right in and took care of things as well as you could have. Perhaps even better. I trust your stay in the woods was profitable, Virgil.''

Virgil shook his head. ''Nah. Just a few possibili-ties.''

''Well, I'm certainly glad you're back, Virgil. You are too old to be running around out in the woods alone. Miss Kristy agrees with me on that, don't you, my dear?''

''I certainly do.''

Virgil shook his finger at the lawyer. ''Dern it, Sam, you speak for yourself. You may be too old, but I'm not.''

Mr. Eldridge turned to Kristy. ''I suppose you'll be going back to school now that Virgil's back?''

She shrugged. ''I . . . I guess so.''

''Well, she's welcome to stay long as she wants to,'' Virgil said, beaming. Mr. Eldridge took his leave after admonishing Virgil again on the dangers of the woods and unseemly people.

''He's sweet.''

''He's a worrywart.'' Virgil tweaked her cheek shyly. ''Oh, honey, you got to stay awhile. I wanted to see you so bad all these years, but shoot, I couldn't ask you. I figured a grown up purty girl like you wouldn't want to waste her time with an old codger like me. But I figured if I had those big crystals, it'd be a good excuse to ask you."

She laughed. "Oh, Granddad, you didn't have to have anything special. I thought maybe you didn't want—the Cunninghams seem to have a problem with saying what we feel, don't we?"

"Reckon we do, honey. I sure am glad you didn't take after your momma too much."

"Me, too, Granddad. Me, too." She was on the point of tears, saddened by all the years wasted because she'd been afraid, because Virgil had been afraid. She suspected that down deep, her father was afraid, too. Afraid his father would reject him again. "Granddad, when I leave . . . well, you'll be okay, won't you?"

He winked at her across the table. "Sure I will, honey. I know now your daddy had to leave." He pointed to the table of crystals. "He worked 'em, but he never loved 'em. Anybody but a stubborn man would of seen that, honey."

She nodded and forced the tears back, then changed the subject. "Where did that crystal John Graves had come from, Granddad?"

"It's one of the ones I'm lookin' for. One of the few I didn't bury. Been in the fruit cellar all these years."

"But—"

"I planted it after I dynamited that hillside so I could see who came lookin' for it. I figured they wasn't too far away from the mine." He frowned off toward the woods. "I sure hope they was workin' for that guru or somebody."

She looked up in surprise. "Why?"

"Well I'd hate to think those boys did it just for meanness. I knew their daddies." Kristy smiled at the innocence of a man whose world was changing too fast around him. She wanted to see vast conspiracies under every rock, but Virgil wanted to see the best in a couple of boys whose fathers he had known.

THEY SPENT the next two days cleaning in the rock shop. Kristy thought it was strange they hadn't seen or heard from Mike, but she supposed, now that Virgil was back, he had no reason to come around. Although she found that thought more than a little depressing, she accepted it. She had managed to convince herself that Mike's great concern for the Cunningham family began and ended with Virgil. She buried her hurt in work, in the endless magic of the crystals. When she felt the time was right, when Virgil got back into his regular routines, she would quietly leave Mount Ida. Leave her grandfather to his devoted Mike.

She had spent long, sleepless hours listening to the owls and the quiet sounds of the forest, wondering what she might have done differently. Wondering if she could have made Mike love her as she loved him. In the end she knew it could not have turned out differently. Mike Ferguson didn't need anyone else. He was self-sufficient. He had his mine, and he had her grandfather.

Late one evening, after they declared the rock shop clean and ready for business, she and Virgil set out for the woods again to look for the hidden crystals. They must have walked five miles—in circles, Kristy thought—and waded the creek several times. They tried the ground near several other smaller creeks that ran into the first creek, until Kristy had no idea where they were. When they started back, she was soaked, covered in burrs and had managed to rip half the front of her T-shirt off. And still they found nothing. She wanted to find the crystals, yet she didn't, because if they found them, there would no longer be a reason for her to stay.

They walked out of the woods just before sunset. The fire of the western sky twinkled back at her from the racks of clean crystals. Mike lounged in a chair in the backyard, a Budweiser beer in his hand. He looked her up and down, that ghost of a smile playing at his lips. "Looks like another fun day in the woods."

Kristy held her head high and walked right past him. "Delightful." As she walked behind the chair, Mike grabbed her wrist. She felt heat surge up her arm.

"Go get cleaned up. We're going to Hot Springs."

As she turned, she noticed he was not dressed in his usual jeans and T-shirt, but was in white duck pants and a deep blue knit shirt. His eyes had deepened to take on the color of the shirt. His skin was like burnished bronze, his hair a deep blond, streaked with sun-bleached gold. She really didn't want to notice. Or care. "I'm going to bed."

He stood. "No, you're going with me. I can take you looking like that, or you can clean up."

She tried to pull away from him, was determined to stay away from him until she left town. "I wouldn't go to Hot Springs with you if you were the last man on earth."

Virgil was slapping his knees and whooping with laughter. "I do believe you met your match, boy."

Mike stood up and pulled her close. "I want you to go to Hot Springs with me."

The faint smell of soap and shampoo and damp, clean hair and after-shave washed over her, and she felt her heart rate kick up a notch—or two or three. "That doesn't sound sincere."

"Please!"

"You are the only man in the world who can make 'please' sound like marching orders."

Virgil walked past them. "You kids go off and have a good time."

"See, Kristy? Orders from your grandfather."

"Coercion. Oh, all right. Where are we going? Someplace where you can murder me and dispose of the body?" With that she dragged her weary bones into the house, took a hot bath and put on her one sundress.

AN HOUR LATER they were sitting in a cozy booth at Coy's in Hot Springs. A booth Kristy thought was a bit too cozy, not to mention too dark, although maybe dark was better than revealing light. The long ride had been made in an uncomfortable silence. She had tried several times to talk about one thing or another, but Mike had given her little more than one-word answers.

After they ordered dinner, Mike leaned back against the booth and stared at her bare shoulders. "So, I guess you'll be going back to school this week."

She wanted very much to drape her napkin over her shoulders. "Maybe."

"Maybe? You either are or you aren't."

"What is this, the inquisition?" Her blood began to boil, although she wasn't sure whether it was in response to his questions or those beautiful blue eyes. He smiled as the waitress put salads in front of them, but the smile faded as soon as the woman walked away.

"I would just like to know what your intentions are."

"My intentions?" She speared a piece of lettuce with her fork and waved it at him. "Good grief, you sound like some irate father grilling a prospective son-in-law."

He shifted nervously. "Virgil thinks you're staying. Says you have the fever."

"Well, maybe I do."

He pointed a finger at her. "Don't you hurt that old man, Kristy. Don't make him promises you can't keep."

"Listen, Mike Ferguson, you may not understand Virgil and me, but Virgil understands Virgil and me. And that's good enough for me."

"Well it's not good enough for me." The waitress set plates of food beside their uneaten salads and winked at Kristy, as though she understood about arguments at dinner. Mike picked up his knife and pointed to her plate. "Might as well eat."

Kristy pushed her food around but ate very little of it. She wanted to tell him she was going to stay forever, but she knew he wouldn't believe her. She wanted to tell him about her feelings, her dreams, but she was afraid he would stare at her, dumbfounded by her words. Or worse, laugh at her. Their attempts at civilized conversation always seemed to end up in arguments. She took a bite of the trout and tried a different tack. "I may just stay here and look after Granddad, help him with the rocks. He could use some help around there."

"Stay for how long? Until he gets used to you being here, comes to depend on you?" His eyes seemed to bore into her very soul. "Until the excitement wears off?"

She slammed down her fork. "Until he doesn't need me anymore, Mike Ferguson. That's how long. Dammit, it is none of your business whether I stay a day or forever, so quit with the bully routine. Okay?"

"I'm making it my business."

"So I've noticed. Well let me tell you something. We aren't all as lucky as you were. You grew up in a beautiful place, you had Virgil to guide you and teach you, and you latched onto what you wanted in life early on. You loved it, and you could make a living at it. Everything fell into place for you.'' She threw her napkin on the table. ''Do you have any idea how rare that kind of luck is these days?''

He cut a piece of his steak but left it on his plate. ''Garrett didn't see things that way. Everybody has choices, and I don't know what mine have to do with this discussion.''

''Lord, are you going to hang onto the sins of my daddy for the rest of your life? He knew what he wanted, just like you did, except he wanted banking. But it's different now. You go away to school—away from community, away from the people you love. You fight the job market, move to some place you don't want to be, worry whether your job will be wiped out tomorrow by some corporate raider. Mike, I know people who would kill to live in these mountains and be able to make a decent living.''

''Including you?''

''Maybe so. But I will not hurt my grandfather. He and I talked about things, and he's okay with whatever I do. If I leave, we will both know it's the right thing to do and the right time to do it.'' She grabbed at the napkin and wadded it into a ball. ''You know, he's not nearly so bitter toward Daddy as you are.'' The reason why suddenly hit her. Mike had seen Virgil's pain through a boy's eyes, without the maturity and age to understand that adults went through emotional upheavals and survived. And he had carried that impression with him all these years. ''Have you ever talked to Granddad about Daddy?''

''No. It would just open up an old wound.''

"But it wouldn't, Mike. The wound is healed."

He leaned closer. "I would love to believe that, Kristy. More than you'll ever know. But we weren't talking about your father—we were talking about you. Mount Ida isn't the fast lane. Most days it doesn't even get up to the speed of the slow lane. You're used to the city, people, shopping, all those things. There is no way you could be happy here."

Kristy couldn't decide if he was trying to convince her or himself of that. "You haven't heard a word I've said. I *hate* the city. I prefer dogs to people, and Mother or Penny have to drag me shopping."

"But there are other drawbacks. Like no careers. I'm sure someone with your vast experience wants a career."

"There are the crystals," she said softly. "Enough beauty and change to last anyone a lifetime. Even a Gemini."

He stared at her for a long moment, then began eating his dinner in silence.

When they set down their knives and forks, Kristy, figuring the evening was shot, decided she might as well ask the hard questions, get everything out in the open. "Why didn't you tell Granddad I was here?"

"I told you."

"You told me something." He looked at her, but his expression was unreadable.

"I went to tell him, but I couldn't find him. That's when I took Merc out looking for him. Maybe I was wrong, okay? But you roared in here and I didn't know you from Adam's off ox, and I didn't know what you wanted."

"What changed your mind? About telling him?" She held her breath, waiting for an answer.

"The night we talked. I guess I decided you really did love him."

"And now?"

"The verdict's not in, yet. It depends on what you do now."

"Mike, you want me to sign a guarantee that I'll stay here forever? In order to stay here for a while? People change, circumstances change."

"Yeah. I know." He called for the check.

They didn't exchange a dozen words on the way home. Kristy thought he probably didn't even remember she was in the truck. It was as if he were fighting some great battle within himself.

When they pulled into Virgil's driveway, he reached over and cupped the back of her neck with his hand. She could feel the strength in him, the heat and something else. She leaned toward him, sure that he would kiss her.

"Go home, Kristy," he said, his voice as soft and silky as a kitten's, "before you break somebody's heart."

She supposed he was talking about Virgil. She started to respond, but he had reached across her and opened the door.

"See you later."

She stood on the driveway looking after him, trying not to cry. "I want you to know, Mike Ferguson, that was the sorriest excuse for a dinner date I have ever been on in my entire life," she called to the disappearing taillights.

Virgil was asleep when she entered the house. She called Penny and asked her to come for the weekend, but Penny was going to San Antonio for the weekend. She would try for the next weekend.

Kristy lay in bed, waiting for sleep, which she knew would be slow in coming. She loved Mike, but she had some hard decisions to make. She could leave and try to forget him. Or stay and try to prove herself to him, hope that in time he would come to trust her and open up to her love. She knew he felt something for her, or at least wanted to feel something—she could see it in his eyes, feel it in his presence—but he kept his shell pulled tightly around him, and no one had the key except her grandfather.

And if it didn't happen? If he didn't return her love? How could she see him, be around him day after day—as inevitably she would—and know she could never have him?

CHAPTER TWELVE

THE WEEK passed slowly. Virgil spent part of his time at the mine but most of it in the woods, searching. Kristy threw herself into her work. She cleaned crystals, the house, the toolshed, the backyard—and anything else she could find. Mike came by twice to check on Virgil, although she suspected they spent long hours together at the mine—discussing things that were not her business, no doubt. He was pleasant but reserved. Kristy found herself counting the hours until Penny got there on Saturday.

Penny arrived shortly after the sun. "I couldn't wait, Kristy, I simply couldn't wait. I want to start a marketing survey right away."

Kristy couldn't help but laugh at her friend's enthusiasm. When Penny stopped talking long enough to survey the house and the rock shop, her smile faded, and Kristy could see doubt written all over her face.

"Is this *it*?"

"No, Penny, this is not it. I mean this is part of it. The mine is up the road." She wrapped her arms around Penny and hugged her. "I am *so* glad to see you. You wouldn't believe what's been going on around here." At that moment Virgil wandered out of the house, and Kristy waved to him. "Granddad, this is my roommate and best friend, Penny."

The old man's face broke into a smile. "Mighty pleased, Miss Penny. You take up a lot of space in Kristy's letters. You seen the scales from the shop, honey?"

"In the backyard. I was weighing some of the new stuff last week."

"You sell this stuff by the pound?" Penny whispered. "Good Lord, Kristy, do you know how much rocks weigh?"

"A lot. Come on, I'll show you the operation." She led Penny to the backyard and began to explain the cleaning process. She was up to the cooking part when she heard the familiar sound of Mike's truck. When he walked around the house, Penny's eyes widened considerably and she elbowed Kristy. Kristy introduced them. Mike was polite but quickly moved to help Virgil unload the tanks.

"I spent half the night going over aerial maps and the topos, Virgil. I think we've been looking too far north." He pulled a map out of his hip pocket and spread it on a table. "See this place? If I remember correctly, the creek has changed course since I was a kid. There are some big boulders that used to sit right in the creek, but now they're high and dry." He gave Kristy a peculiar look when he mentioned the rocks. "I think we ought to try it. There's an old logging road that goes in here." He jabbed at the map. "We can drive most of the way."

Virgil's eyes twinkled. "Well, let's go, boy."

Kristy walked over and looked at the map. "Let me go put on my jeans. Penny, do you have any old clothes?"

"Sure."

Kristy almost laughed. Penny's idea of old clothes would be designer Levi's jeans instead of Ralph Lauren casuals. "We'll be ready in a minute."

Mike folded the map with slow deliberation. "This is a real rough part of the mountain. We'll check it out. If we find anything, we'll come get you."

Kristy looked around for a blunt instrument. "Too rough for the ladies, Mike?"

He smiled. "I didn't mean that, Kristy. I just meant there's no reason to waste everyone's time on speculation."

"I know exactly what you meant, Mike," she said and stalked off toward the shop, Penny close on her heels.

"Is that hunk your idea of just another good old boy, Kristy?"

Kristy glared as the men loaded shovels into the truck. Mercury flew into the truck bed and hung over the side, smiling at her as if he, too, were pleased with the situation. "I hope you run across a five-hundred-pound bunny, Merc. One that eats ungrateful, wretched hounds instead of grass."

Penny nudged her. "I said, is that your idea of a good old—"

"Good old boys come in many sizes and shapes, Penny, but believe me, Mike Ferguson is a good old boy."

Penny grinned. "Uh-huh. Kristy, I can't believe you've been here having adventures and falling in love, and you didn't even bother to call me. How could you?"

"I was *not* falling in love. I couldn't possibly love a man who is so irritating and annoying and who is, beyond a shadow of a doubt, a Virgo, and who is—oh, Penny, what am I going to do?''

"You go for it, Kristy. Kidnap him, do whatever it takes." As if that bit of advice took care of everything, Penny moved on to business matters. "Is he the one with the big mine? Lord, he must have scads of money."

"I'm sure he does. Not that I care. Now, do you want to know about these stupid rocks or don't you."

"Testy, testy. I want to hear everything that's happened to you since you left Austin. Not one word left out, Kristy."

As they washed crystals, Kristy told her friend everything that had happened. Well, almost everything. She left out the kiss—after all what was one lousy kiss? She left out the disastrous dinner in Hot Springs, and she left out all of her feelings about the one lousy kiss and the disastrous dinner. When she'd finished, Penny was quiet for a long time, as if she suspected much of what Kristy had not told her.

"Who would believe anyone could have that much excitement in a place like this? Okay, we'll get your personal life straightened out later. It sounds to me like your basic misunderstanding. Right now, we have to find the big crystals. Now we are going to sit down, and you are going to tell me everything you remember about your summers here as a kid. It's all a matter of logic and recall and putting the parts together."

"I've tried that, Penny."

"Kristy, you do not have a logical bone in your body. Now sit."

Although Kristy thought it the height of silliness, she leaned back in the lawn chair, closed her eyes and began to summon up all those memories from long ago. It was like reliving the past—she and Virgil and Chester would set out in early morning, their pockets crammed with cans of Vienna sausages and soda crackers. Sometimes Mike would come along, but he always seemed annoyed that she was there. They would spend the morning wandering and digging for crystals. Once, they hit a pocket of clusters so tiny and delicate that Kristy thought they must have been made by fairies.

At noon they would eat their lunch and drink from a cold clear spring or creek. Kristy remembered pulling broken soda crackers from her pocket. Many days, if it was within walking distance, they would eat at a place where the big rocks were.

"One rock looked like Dumbo," Kristy said dreamily, a smile on her face. "I would climb to the top, sit on Dumbo's head and eat my lunch. If Mikey was there, he'd laugh at me. He said it couldn't be Dumbo because it didn't have ears or a trunk. But that rock was always Dumbo to me."

"What else did you see. Besides Dumbo?" Penny asked softly.

"The old pine tree, black and scarred. Then later it was a stump."

"Which way do we go, Kristy?"

"Follow the moss on the trees. I blazed an Indian trail to Dumbo once, marked the trees and followed the moss. Moss always grows on the north side of the trees, you know."

"How did you know which moss? I mean which trees?"

"The sun. At noon it was always between two hills. I could stand and sight from the last marked tree—" She sat up straight. "That's it, Penny. Granddad always said you found your way by the trees. But I never could tell one tree from the other. When I got to the fence and up the hill, I looked at the far hills. Come on, I'll bet there are still some marks on the older trees."

She grabbed a shovel out of the shed. "Wait, I'll leave a note. I guess this will show Mike Ferguson a thing or two." She ran into the house, scrawled a note telling them to follow the marks on the trees to Dumbo and stuck the scrap of paper to the back door—which was a waste of time because Mike and Virgil probably wouldn't be back before dark.

Kristy tried not to think about what she was doing or where she was going. She was that little girl again, marking a trail so she could go sit on Dumbo when Virgil and Chester were too busy to go. She headed west. Virgil owned forty acres where the house sat, and the hardwoods and pines were mature and not crowded like the replanted forests. Virgil had thinned his woods of scrub trees, but he would never cut a mature tree. She walked and looked at the trees.

Suddenly, Penny squealed. "Look."

The mark on the oak tree was faint and had almost sealed itself over the years, but the crude heart and arrow was there. The growing seasons had obliterated the names, but with a sudden flash of memory, Kristy knew she had carved "Mikey and Kristy" on the tree.

"A heart? Real authentic Indian markings, Kristy."

"I was twelve, okay?"

"Okay. Lead on, Tonto."

It all began to come back clearly, and Kristy found herself walking a straight line, hardly looking at the trees now. When they came to the sagging, rusted fence at the end of Virgil's property, they were facing a steep hillside covered with slender, half-grown pine trees. A paper company had logged this hill the last summer she was here. She had sat on the fence and watched the men fell the pine trees and carry them off on their huge trucks. She'd cried for days over all those poor trees. "This is the hillside, Penny. We're going the right way." She just hoped they were going to the right spot.

"The question is, how do we get through all these trees? Why do they plant them so close?"

"Economics, Penny."

When they finally got to the top of the hill, she saw the two blue-green peaks in the distance. "There they are, Penny. We hang a left, and the creek is right down there. Good grief, no wonder we couldn't find the place. We've been looking too far away." They pushed their way through the young pines and underbrush, skirted the hill and skidded down a deep draw. When they came to a stop, they were in a creek bed that was dry except for a few pools of deep, clear water. The place was hidden from everything and everyone, unless you knew exactly where it was. One side of the creek was a sandbar. A few scraggly elm trees grew along the sides, leaning until they met in the middle. A huge boulder sat in the sandbar, like a giant animal protecting its lair.

"That's Dumbo, Penny. See him?"

"Geez, Kristy, I have to agree with Mike on that one. Doesn't look anything like an elephant."

"Virgil always said Dumbo was sitting on a nest."

"So, let's find the eggs." They began to dig in the soft sand around the boulder. The day was warm, and the sweat poured from them as they took turns digging with the shovel.

Penny wiped her brow. "What if they're forty feet deep?"

"I don't think so. They didn't have backhoes back then. Virgil would have used a shovel to bury them."

"How in the world did Virgil ever get them to a place like this? There aren't any roads."

"They used mules in those days, Penny." She dug as fast as she dared, being careful not to damage anything she hit. When they found nothing at three feet, Kristy moved to another spot. "Just be grateful we're working in sand and not that hard, rocky ground that's around the house." When the shovel struck something, she threw it aside and began to search with her hands. Penny joined her, and the sand flew out of the hole. They uncovered what looked like an old wooden crate, with railroad ties over it for reinforcement. The top of the crate had rotted through, and sand had drifted into the dark hole left there. Kristy reached down and pushed away loose sand until she retrieved a long, clay-covered object.

She couldn't see one bit of quartz showing, but she knew it was one of the crystals. The clay was hard and dry, so they peeled off all they could, and she could feel the hard edges of the prism. "Let's get it into the water."

They carried their find to one of the pools of water and carefully lowered it. Kristy was certain the crystal was not indigenous to this sandbar. It *had* been buried there. She took off her T-shirt, ripped a piece from the back and began to wipe the softened clay away.

As they watched, the point appeared. A perfect point—it formed a perfect triangle at the top. "It's as big as my leg, Penny. I can't believe it! I'll bet it's water clear."

The pool of water turned red and cloudy with the clay, and they moved the big crystal to another pool and gently rubbed at the remaining clay. Even under the water, the crystal began to catch fire from the sun, and when they lifted it out, they both gasped. The whole thing was a single point, a good two feet long, at least four inches across. The sides were as smooth as glass, and the crystal was just as clear, except for an inch or so of milky white quartz at the bottom. It sparkled and glittered like a fine diamond in the afternoon sun.

Penny swallowed hard. "No wonder these things cause such a stir. I've never seen anything like it."

"We found them, Penny. We found them!" They carried the crystal, which must have weighed forty pounds, back to the sandbar and laid it down. "I'm going to squirm down into that crate and hand the rest out."

"No you aren't, I am." Before Kristy could stop her, Penny had moved one of the ties enough for her to wriggle down into the crate. She had passed up three clusters when, without warning, the sides of the rotted crate gave way and the ties collapsed around her. Penny screamed as sand avalanched down on her. Kristy dug furiously until she had cleared her friend's head and arms. "Are you okay, Penny? Penny?"

"Okay. I'm okay." Pain creased her face. "Maybe a broken leg."

Kristy started digging, murmuring assurances the whole time, but within minutes, she knew she needed help. "Hang on, Penny. I'll be back before you know it." She scrambled up the steep side of the draw, then along the ridge and down through the young pines. Before she got to the fence, she heard a dog howl. Mercury. Mike and Virgil must be back. She called to them and kept running. Just as she came out of a thick stand of pines, Mercury appeared, running full tilt. Unable to stop, he smashed into her, and they went down in a tangle.

Mike burst out of the trees with Virgil close behind. Kristy caught her breath long enough to tell them about Penny. Then they were all tearing through the woods.

AN HOUR LATER Kristy and Mike sat in the emergency room waiting area. The doctor thought Penny had escaped with a broken leg and a few cuts and scratches. Virgil had muttered something about Clyde and a heart attack and had disappeared down the hall. Kristy searched for something to say to Mike. "I thought you'd be gone all day."

Mike sat with his elbows on his knees, studying the floor. "Virgil and I had a little talk on our way to the site."

"Oh?"

"About Garrett. You were right, Kristy."

She held her breath. "That's a first," she said lightly.

"You were right about a lot of things. I had no right to keep you away from Virgil."

Her breath came unevenly. "But I understand why you did it, Mike. And I was wrong about more things than I was right about. So how come you came back so soon today? Forget a tool?''

He turned to her and cupped her face in his hands. "I came back for you, Kristy. To tell you what a jerk I've been.''

"You did?'' She felt a surge of warmth flood through her body.

"I love you, Kristy, and I can't let you go back to school. And if you get tired of me and bored with this life, then you'll just have to leave, but for right now, I want you here.'' His lips brushed against hers. "If you'll have me, stubborn as I am.''

She pushed him away. "Here? You mean, like—''

"Like wife, Kristy. Married.''

Kristy thought she might very well drop dead from shock. "But I thought after that awful dinner—''

"I wanted you to say something, Kristy. I wanted some encouragement, some indication that you felt the same things I did.''

"Well *you* could have said something.'' She tried to ignore his warm breath in her ear, afraid she was so addled she wasn't hearing him right. "But...but...I can't possibly marry a Virgo. It would never work.''

He smiled and traced kisses down her jawline. "But I'm not a Virgo. I'm a Sagittarius.''

"A Sagi...really?'' She couldn't think with his kisses teasing her throat. "Opposites. Why didn't you tell me?''

"You never asked. Opposites? I guess we are at that.'' His lips touched hers, and she thought she would melt.

"Well, opposites *have* been known to work,'' she murmured as his kiss deepened. She reached up to touch his face, his hair, to explore the hard muscles of his back, and she thought she might just explode from all the emotions and feelings coursing through her. When he suddenly pulled away, she gasped. ''What—''

''I almost forgot. I have something for you. In the truck.''

''But Penny—''

''She's in good hands.'' They walked out into the bright fall day, and he took a cardboard box out of the truck bed. ''For you. Kind of to seal things.''

She was touched by his sudden shyness. She opened the box, and when she'd pulled away the wads of newspaper, the double-terminator formation she'd admired in his wholesale shop drew in the late afternoon sun and gave it back to her a thousand times over. ''Oh, Mike— don't you think it's a little large for an engagement ring?''

He put the box aside and growled. ''You always were a smart aleck.''

''I love it, Mike. And I love you.'' The words sounded strange and wonderful. Just as she reached up to kiss him, Penny hobbled out the door on crutches, Virgil at her side. He whooped and pointed at them. ''I knew it, I knew it. But you got a lifetime for that stuff. We got us some crystals to dig.''

''Now Virgil,'' Penny was explaining. ''We need to talk tax shelters and charitable trusts and a few other things. I have to check on capital gains, but maybe they don't count where rocks are concerned.''

Kristy laughed and snuggled closer to Mike. ''She'll have Granddad incorporated and on the big board before sundown.''

Mike wrapped her in his arms. His kiss was sweet and gentle. "Maybe it'll keep them busy enough that I can have you to myself *after* sundown."

EPILOGUE

KRISTY STOOD in the doorway of the metal building, watching Mike and her grandfather wrestle the last of the lost crystals onto a table. As usual, they hadn't bothered to turn on the lights. When she flipped the switch, she took a deep breath and held it. She had helped clean the rocks and make room for them, but she was still not prepared for the sight now that the shimmering treasures were all in one place.

She walked into the room as if she were entering a great cathedral. All around her single points and clusters of every size glittered in the light from overhead. She tried to think of words to describe the effect, but words were not sufficient. She stopped beside a large cluster that bristled with smoky quartz points, their delicate gray color as exquisite in its own way as the clear specimens. Each one she looked at was more beautiful, more perfect, than the last.

When she looked up, Mike and Virgil were watching her.

"They're yours, Kristy, honey." Virgil said, "To remember your old granddaddy by."

Kristy felt the tears well. "Oh, Granddad, do you think I need some old rock to remember you?"

"You hear that, boy? Some old rock? I like to get myself killed, and she calls these things some old rock?"

Kristy wiped her face and laughed. "I've become jaded by all this beauty." She walked over and gave her grandfather a hug and a kiss. "I'd love to keep a few, Granddad, but they're yours. If you don't want to keep them or sell them, maybe they belong in museums for people to enjoy. Can't you just see them scattered all over this country, with a brass plate beside every one of them?—Courtesy of Virgil Cunningham, Cunningham Mine, Mount Ida, Arkansas.''

Virgil's face lit up. "Well, now, I reckon that'd be right nice, wouldn't it? Show a few of them furriners just what we got in this state.''

"I talked to Daddy."

Virgil's smile faded. "That right?"

"That's right." She glanced at Mike. He nodded encouragement. "He thought maybe, when he came down for the wedding next month, he might look around for some land to buy.''

"Why would your daddy want any land around here?"

"Oh, no special reason. He's thinking about retiring.''

Virgil frowned. "That boy ain't old enough to retire.''

"Oh, Granddad, he's got scads of money. He's very good at being a banker. And when you have scads of money, you can retire whenever you want.''

"Well, I guess that'd be all right. But a man needs work to occupy his mind.''

"Well, he's been looking into the industrial quartz market. Says it looks sound for some years to come."

A smile wiped away Virgil's frown. "He has, has he?"

"He has. Now if you will excuse us, Mike and I need to concoct a plan for keeping mother away from here till five minutes before the wedding. Otherwise, she will organize us all to death." She took Mike's arm, and they left Virgil to his "rocks." "Oh, Mike, do you really think Daddy and Granddad can get back together?"

He wrapped his arms around her and kissed her soundly. "Yeah, I think they can. You and I will see to it. I think I owe Garrett that much, after what I've said about him all these years. By the way, have you decided on anything more specific than the middle of October for a wedding date?"

"Ummm," she murmured as he kissed her eyes, then her nose. "Seventeenth. I finished my chart last night. It's the perfect day. Happiness assured." She flung the back of her hand against her forehead in a dramatic gesture. "Oh, Mike," she cried, "what would I have done if you'd turned out to be a Virgo?"

He twirled an imaginary mustache. "I would have burned your charts, carried you away and *forced* you to marry me." She laughed, and his lips touched hers before she could explain that she had already burned her charts. With him she knew what her future held.

HARLEQUIN
Romance

Coming Next Month

#3109 EVERY WOMAN'S DREAM Bethany Campbell
Cal Buchanan's photograph landed on Tess's desk like manna from heaven. It
would guarantee the success of the calendar project that could launch Tess in New
York's advertising world. Only things don't work out quite that way—there
are complications....

#3110 FAIR TRIAL Elizabeth Duke
They come from two different worlds, Tanya Barrington and Simon Devlin, two
lawyers who have to work together on a case. Their clashes are inevitable—and
their attraction to each other is undeniable.

#3111 THE GIRL HE LEFT BEHIND Emma Goldrick
Molly and Tim were childhood friends, and he never knew that he'd broken Molly's
heart when he married her cousin. When Tim turns up on Molly's doorstep with his
daughter, asking for help, Molly takes them in despite the pain they bring her. And
the joy . . .

#3112 AN IMPOSSIBLE PASSION Stephanie Howard
Fayiz Davidian's job offer comes just when Giselle needs it, and if he thinks she'll
refuse just because she finds him arrogant and overbearing, he's dead wrong. She
always rises to a challenge!

#3113 FIRST COMES MARRIAGE Debbie Macomber
Janine Hartman's grandfather and Zach Thomas have merged their companies.
Now Gramps wants to arrange another kind of merger—a wedding between his
unwilling granddaughter and an equally unwilling Zach!

#3114 HIDDEN HEART Jessica Steele
To protect her sister and family, Mornay shoulders the blame when wealthy
industrialist Brad Kendrick wrongly accuses her of being the hit-and-run driver
who'd landed him in the hospital. She never suspects that her heart will
become involved....

Available in March wherever paperback books are sold, or through
Harlequin Reader Service:

In the U.S.
P.O. Box 1397
Buffalo, N.Y.
14240-1397

In Canada
P.O. Box 603
Fort Erie, Ontario
L2A 5X3

COMING IN 1991 FROM
HARLEQUIN SUPERROMANCE:

Three abandoned orphans,
one missing heiress!

Dying millionaire Owen Byrnside receives an
anonymous letter informing him that twenty-six years
ago, his son, Christopher, fathered a daughter. The
infant was abandoned at a foundling home that
subsequently burned to the ground, destroying all
records. Three young women could be Owen's long-
lost granddaughter, and Owen is determined to track
down each of them! Read their stories in

#434 HIGH STAKES (available January 1991)
#438 DARK WATERS (available February 1991)
#442 BRIGHT SECRETS (available March 1991)

Three exciting stories of intrigue and romance by
veteran Superromance author Jane Silverwood.

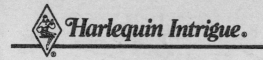

They went in through the terrace door. The house was dark, most of the servants were down at the circus, and only Nelbert's hired security guards were in sight. It was child's play for Blackheart to move past them, the work of two seconds to go through the solid lock on the terrace door. And then they were creeping through the darkened house, up the long curving stairs, Ferris fully as noiseless as the more experienced Blackheart.

They stopped on the second floor landing. "What if they have guns?" Ferris mouthed silently.

Blackheart shrugged. "Then duck."

"How reassuring," she responded. Footsteps directly above them signaled that the thieves were on the move, and so should they be.

For more romance, suspense and adventure, read Harlequin Intrigue. Two exciting titles each month, available wherever Harlequin Books are sold.

INTA-1